Lexie wa̶̶̶̶̶̶̶̶̶er

And if there was a̶̶̶̶ who could kiss better than Josh, God bless the woman who found him. Josh not only had a beautiful mouth, he knew how to use it.

She wanted that mouth on her, too.

Everything masculine about him had everything feminine in her waving white flags of surrender. No doubt about it, he was the perfect fun, wild, temporary guy to end her long bout with celibacy. He was definitely Mr. Fling.

The waitress brought the check, and Josh quickly grabbed it, scribbling his name across the bottom.

When Lexie protested, Josh put his hand up. "A cowboy can't let a lady buy his beer. Think of the ribbing I'd get around the campfire."

"Like you already get for getting bitten on the behind by a snake?"

"Exactly." He gave her a sexy, heart-melting grin. "Wanna see my scar?"

Josh's tone was light, but there was no mistaking the note of arousal in his voice, or the underlying meaning behind his question. Taking the plunge, Lexie took his hand and pulled him to his feet. Smiling wickedly, she answered, "Yeah, I do…."

Dear Reader,

Sometimes the more we try to plan things, the worse they turn out. If I plan an outdoor cookout, I can almost guarantee it will rain. Or I'll discover, in the middle of preparing a recipe, that I'm missing a key ingredient—like spaghetti for Pasta Primavera. (Yes, it happened!) So how could I not give my hero and heroine the same problem? Both Josh and Lexie have specific plans for their future, plans that don't include the other. Only, the instant they meet, those plans start unraveling....

As for me, I've found a great way to relieve some of the stress. I call it the "ish" rule. When my husband asks, "When are we planning to leave?" I answer, "Nine-ish." (Nine-ish is anywhere between 8:45 and 10:30.) When my son asks, "What's for dinner?" I answer, "Something Italian-ish." (This can be anything from pizza to Taco Bell with a side of marinara sauce.) Believe me, not having plans carved in stone helps— but Josh and Lexie will have to figure that out for themselves.

I love to hear from readers! You can contact me at 875 Lawrenceville-Suwanee Rd., Ste. 310-PMB 131, Lawrenceville, GA 30043, or e-mail me through my Web site at www.JacquieD.com, where you can enter my monthly contest and find out all my latest releases.

Happy reading,

Jacquie D'Alessandro

Books by Jacquie D'Alessandro

HARLEQUIN DUETS
56—NAKED IN NEW ENGLAND

IN OVER HIS HEAD
Jacquie D'Alessandro

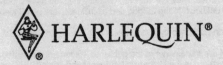

HARLEQUIN®

TORONTO • NEW YORK • LONDON
AMSTERDAM • PARIS • SYDNEY • HAMBURG
STOCKHOLM • ATHENS • TOKYO • MILAN • MADRID
PRAGUE • WARSAW • BUDAPEST • AUCKLAND

This book is dedicated with my love and gratitude to
Michelle, Steven and Lindsay Grossman, for all the good times we've shared,
and those still to come. And, as always, to my wonderful husband, Joe,
who, in spite of not being a cowboy, still lassoed my heart.
And to my son, Christopher, aka Lasso, Jr.

Thank you to Carol Painter, President of the Manhattan Area
Chamber of Commerce, for answering my questions about Montana,
and to Dr. J. Whitfield Gibbons, Professor of Ecology, University of
Georgia/Savannah River Ecology Lab for sharing his expertise about snake bites.
Thanks also to Brenda Chin, Damaris Rowland, Wendy Etherington, Jenni Grizzle,
Kay and Jim Johnson, Lea and Art D'Alessandro, Jeannie Pierannunzi,
and a special thank-you to Denise Forbes and Pat Pruitt
for the great book signings.
And thanks to all the wonderful readers
who have taken the time to write me.

ISBN 0-373-69117-3

IN OVER HIS HEAD

Copyright © 2003 by Jacquie D'Alessandro.

Printed in U.S.A.

Prologue

LEXIE WEBSTER looked at the vast array of purses in the department store display case and sighed. Turning toward her best friend she said, "Darla, I don't need a new purse."

"Of course you don't," Darla agreed, pulling her toward the designer handbags. "I do. What *you* need is sex."

The sales associate glanced at them, and Lexie shot Darla "the look." "No, what I *need* is to get back to the resort. I have work to do."

Darla held up a brown leather bag for inspection. "It's Sunday. Your day off."

"I'm booked to teach a private scuba lesson at three o'clock."

Darla set the brown bag back on the counter and crossed her arms over her chest. Fashionably dressed in a pale blue pin-striped Ralph Lauren suit, her shoulder-length tawny hair pulled back in a chic chignon, Darla looked, as she always did, as though she'd just stepped off a page from *Vogue*. Lexie looked down at her own attire and winced. Plain white tank top, faded jeans, and Nikes that had seen better days. It wasn't that she didn't like to dress up—she did. But one hardly wore Ralph Lauren to read the newspaper on the deck, and that's what she'd been doing when Darla had come by after spending the morning with a potential buyer and commandeered her to go shopping.

"That's exactly the problem, Lex," Darla said. "You're working yourself into the ground. You need to take some time for *you*."

"You worked today," Lexie pointed out.

"I'm a real estate agent. We work on Sundays. Except when we need to have a serious conversation with our best friend. Then we go shopping and talk."

Uh-oh. Based on Darla's earlier "what you need is sex" comment, Lexie had a pretty good idea where this conversation was headed. "Look, Darla, I know you mean well, but—"

"No buts. Consider this an intervention." Darla planted her hands on her hips and jutted out her chin at a stubborn angle. With determination glinting in her green eyes, she reminded Lexie of Xena: Warrior Princess—or at least Xena's beautiful, tawny-haired, Ralph Lauren-clad sister. "Here's the deal, Lex. I'm not letting you leave the handbag department until this is settled."

"Great. I wouldn't mind so much if you'd picked the shoe department instead," Lexie joked.

Genuine concern softened Darla's fierce expression and she reached out to clasp Lexie's hands. "Lexie, I'm worried about you. You're working yourself to the bone."

"I'm working extra hours because this is the resort's busiest time of the year. I have to take on the extra work while it's available. You know I need the money. When that plot of land I've been saving for comes on the market, I'll need all the cash I can lay my hands on to buy it." In an effort to erase the worry still puckering Darla's brow, she teased, "You realize the only reason I keep you around is because I want that land and you've got real estate connections."

"And the only reason I keep you around is because

you get me great discounts at the resort's spa." Darla's eyes narrowed. "You know, the *spa*—a place where people go to alleviate their stress. I would suggest you go, but in your case, more drastic measures are needed. A simple massage and a facial just aren't going to cut it. You need a full-fledged, hot, steamy—"

"—sauna?"

"Fling." When Lexie didn't reply, Darla plunged on. "I don't even want to think about how long it's been since you've had sex."

Eleven months, two weeks and three days. Lexie didn't want to think about it, either. And she sure wasn't going to add fuel to the fire by reminding Darla.

"You're under a lot of stress, Lex."

"I'm busy."

"Working yourself to death for that piece of land."

"Because I want a home. A *real* home. On that cove."

"I understand. And I'll let you know the instant the owner is interested in selling. But in the meantime you have *got* to loosen up."

As much as Lexie hated to admit it, Darla had a point. "I guess I have been sort of tense lately."

"*Sort of* tense?" Darla shook her head and made tsking noises. "You're a volcano on the verge of eruption. If I looked up 'tense' in the dictionary, your picture would be right there. You need stress relief like no one I've ever met before. And believe me, the best stress reliever in the world is sex. Why do you think I'm always so relaxed?"

"I thought it was all that time you spent in the spa with my discount."

Darla laughed. "Facials and massages are great, but sex is better. Trust me. A couple of bouts of steamy sex and you'll be a new woman. Good Lord, your body must be literally starved from all this celibacy. You are primed for a fling."

Lexie sighed. "Maybe. But I don't want a serious relationship."

Darla wrinkled her small nose. "Of course you don't. Relationships are highly overrated, as you and I both well know. I'm talking strictly a fling. No-strings-attached sex to get you out of your rut. Fling rules apply."

"And what are those?"

"There's only three." She released Lexie's hands and counted the **rules** off on her fingers. "It has to be fun, wild and temporary. Think you can handle that?"

Fun, wild. She hadn't done anything like that in a long time. And temporary? She'd *never* done that—at least not in a premeditated fashion. It sounded... intriguing. And exciting in a way that had her hibernating hormones peeking open their eyelids.

"You know what, Darla? I think I can handle that."

Darla's smile lit up her heart-shaped face. "Excellent. Now all we have to do is find the right man."

Lexie groaned. "That's going to be a challenge. It's not as if terrific guys are falling at my feet."

"You don't need a 'terrific' guy. We're not looking for husband material. He only has to be fling-worthy." She leaned closer, as if she were about to impart some great secret. "You're just using him for sex."

A grin tugged at Lexie's lips. "He might not appreciate that."

Darla straightened then favored her with her best give-me-a-break look. "Yeah, right. Men just hate it when attractive women seduce them. Especially women who aren't expecting hearts, flowers and diamond rings. Believe me, we won't have trouble finding a willing man."

"But I don't want just *any* guy."

"Don't worry," Darla said. "You'll know the guy when you meet him."

"How?"

A devilish gleam sparkled in Darla's eyes. "He'll be the one you can't keep your eyes—or hands—off. Once you see him, just let nature do the rest. Remember—fun, wild and temporary." Darla held out her hand. "Agreed?"

Lexie took a deep breath. Darla was right. It was time to take a break from her all-work-and-no-play life. Since her breakup with Tony almost a year ago, she'd lived like a monk.

Well, she wasn't a monk. She was a twenty-eight-year-old woman who badly needed some *fun, wild* and *temporary* in her life. And thanks to Darla's pep talk, she was primed and ready to take the plunge.

Grasping Darla's hand, Lexie shook on it. "Agreed."

WITH HIS HEAVY canvas duffel digging into his shoulder, Josh Maynard watched the taxicab that had just deposited him at his destination disappear into the distance. Pushing his favorite Stetson back a few inches, he turned in a slow circle to survey his unfamiliar surroundings.

Whew. He sure wasn't in Montana anymore. Not a mountain or stately pine tree in sight. Instead flat green land greeted his gaze and palm trees soared toward the cloudless azure sky. And man, it was hot. And humid. This heavy, damp Florida air surrounded him like a sticky, wet blanket. The moist heat radiating upward from the asphalt made him feel as if he were rotating on a barbecue spit.

He turned his attention to the hotel that would be his home for the next few weeks. Bright turquoise lettering on the gleaming white stucco exterior proclaimed Whispering Palms Resort. Colorful pink and orange blooms climbed up wooden trellises, and what seemed like hundreds of flowers and shrubs dotted the verdant lawn and well-manicured grounds.

But the resort was more than just a place of beauty, which is why he'd chosen it. Based on the Internet research he'd conducted and the enthusiastic recommendation of his travel agent, the Whispering Palms boasted a reputation of running the most comprehensive water activities program in the area. Their staff was reported to be professional, with impressive credentials.

He also liked that the resort was located a bit off the beaten track—close enough to Miami to be convenient, but far away from all the crowds. And he'd liked the more intimate size of the place. He hadn't wanted one of those megaresorts with thousands of guest rooms.

He breathed deeply and his nostrils twitched at the unusual scents. Not a whiff of horseflesh, leather saddles or rodeo arena anywhere. This air smelled... tropical. Fruity and sweet, with the underlying tang of the ocean. He rocked back on his boot heels. Nope, this place was nuthin' like home.

But that was the whole point.

He eyeballed the minimally dressed guests wandering in and out of the resort's open-air entrance, then glanced down at his own attire. No doubt about it, he looked as out of place as a tumbleweed among hothouse flowers. His long-sleeved denim shirt and Wranglers would definitely have to go. He'd stood outside here less than two minutes and already an uncomfortable trickle of perspiration dampened his back.

His gaze lowered to his feet, and he heaved a sigh. His beloved Tony Lamas would have to go as well, he supposed. Not much call for boots on the beach. Good thing he'd bought himself a pair of Nikes before leaving Montana, although he couldn't say he much cared for them. Still, a man had to do—or in this case, wear—what a man had to wear.

He'd waited a long time to start on this adventure, and he wasn't about to let a little thing like trading in his comfortable Western wear for surfer-boy beach clothes scare him off. No sir. Sure the obstacles were high, but he'd conquered higher. Had the gold belt buckles from the Professional Rodeo Cowboys Association—and the scars—to prove it. Except for that last competition, of course. Damn it, coming in second to Wes Handly still chapped his hide. If only—

Josh sliced off the irritating thought before it could take root. That part of his life was over. He'd hung up his spurs and it was time to conquer new worlds. Such as this beachy, suntan-oiled, palm-treed, flowery, mountainless, oceany-smelling...place.

Inhaling a fruity-scented resolute breath, he adjusted his Stetson, settled his duffel higher on his shoulder, then walked toward the entrance of the resort, his senses trying to take in all the new sights, sounds and smells at once.

A huge birdcage dominated the parquet-floored lobby. The largest parrot Josh had ever seen—not that he'd seen many—sat perched on a wooden swing, its long, bright red, yellow, and green tail feathers cutting a colorful yard-long downward swath. Big-leafed plants sprang from porcelain urns painted with tropical scenes featuring flamingos and multihued fish. Salmon-colored walls glowed behind the long, dark green granite reception desk. Craning his neck to look beyond the reception area, he caught a glimpse of a sparkling pool, then the white beach and blue ocean beyond. A pleasant breeze blew through the lobby, cooling his overheated skin.

By God, Dad would have loved this place. The bright colors, the salty air, the squawk of gulls. And wouldn't he have just gotten the biggest kick out of that huge parrot? A sharp pang of regret stabbed Josh, halting his steps, hitching his breath. His fingers clenched around his duffel strap, the coarse material and metal clasp bit-

-ing into his palm. Damn it, would the grief ever stop sneaking up on him? Hitting him like a bull's kick to the head? Most likely not. But maybe after he'd accomplished what he'd come here to do...maybe then the ache would lessen.

He looked out toward the sandy beach and deep blue water and swallowed hard. Yup, Dad had wanted his whole life to come to a place like this, but he'd never even gotten the chance to see the ocean. His dad's crinkle-eyed smiling face rose in his mind's eye, and his raspy voice echoed through his mind, so clearly it seemed as if Bill Maynard stood next to him. *When I retire from ranchin', I'm gonna satisfy this itch of a wanderlust, son. Learn to sail, then buy me a boat. Go places and see things I've only ever read about or seen on TV. I'm gonna sail around the Mediterranean. Eat whatever I catch for dinner.*

A ghost of a smile tugged at the corners of Josh's mouth as he recalled teasing his dad. *Eat whatever you catch for dinner? You'd better add "learn deep-sea fishing" to your list of things to do, Dad, or you're gonna starve. Won't be the same as pullin' trout from a mountain stream.*

I plan to learn, son. And you can learn with me. I can picture it now. The two of us sailin' on the crystal-clear water, grillin' up the day's catch.

I look forward to it, Dad. But I'll bring along some steaks. Just in case.

A loud parrot squawk roused Josh from his thoughts and he resolutely tucked his memories away. It was time to check in, unpack his bag, throw on some beachwear, and start fulfilling the dream Dad had instilled in him three decades ago.

Squaring his shoulders, Josh approached the registration desk. He would set about conquering the seven seas, just as he'd conquered the inside of countless ro-

deo arenas. With hard work, determination, perseverance and heart. *Don't worry, Dad. I'll see all those places
you wanted to see, all those places we talked about. And that
sail we dreamed of taking together? Well, it's as good as done.*

Of course, in spite of all the reading he'd done about
sailing, he'd still need to start with the basics. But it
shouldn't prove too difficult. The staff here was top-
notch, and he was an intelligent man. Had the college
degree to prove it. And he was a world-class athlete.
Had those gold belt buckles to prove that.

His gaze skimmed over the turquoise pool, then settled on the azure ocean beyond. A ripple of unease
trickled down his spine, but he firmly pushed it aside.
Nothing to worry about. The waters here were adver-
tised as calm and crystal-clear.

Besides, how the hell hard could it be to learn to
swim?

LEXIE SMILED and waved goodbye to her class of young
swimming students. "See you tomorrow," she called
after them. The youngest, four-year-old Amy, turned
and blew Lexie a kiss.

Lexie snatched the invisible offering from the air.
"Got it!" she said, planting the "kiss" on her cheek,
much to the child's delight. She would definitely miss
adorable Amy when her family left the Whispering
Palms at the end of the week.

Hoisting herself out of the pool, she grabbed her
towel and dabbed at the water clinging to her skin as
her gaze wandered over the beachfront landscape she
loved. Dozens of people frolicked in the gentle surf
while a group of youngsters built an enormous sand
castle. Parents, singles, honeymooners and teenagers
reclined on aqua-and-yellow-striped lounge chairs,

sunning themselves, reading, napping, chatting, sipping frothy tropical drinks, complete with paper umbrellas, each enjoying their vacation in their own way.

As Activities and Sports Director at the resort, she took great pride in the wide variety of activities the Whispering Palms offered its guests. Water sports ranged from tame snorkeling and inner-tubing, to the more adventurous sailing, waterskiing, kayaking, scuba diving and parasailing. Was exercise your thing? Aerobics were offered twice daily. Biking? Single and tandem bikes were available, as well as tricycles for the tykes. Trampoline? Got it. Beachcombing walks? Check. Water or beach volleyball? You betcha.

Yes, indeed, everything an "in need of rest and relaxation" vacationer could possibly want was available at the Whispering Palms, and pride filled Lexie that she'd played a major role in setting up, then implementing, the activities program. Of course, now that the tourist season was ending, things would slow down until they picked up again around Thanksgiving. She'd miss the hectic pace and the jovial crowds, and she'd definitely miss the additional money she earned during the summer by working evening and early morning hours at the resort's Camp Kid's Club or giving private swimming and scuba lessons. She squirreled away every dollar she could, waiting for her piece of heaven to be listed for sale.

An image of the palm-shaded, waterfront cove she'd fallen in love with rose in her mind's eye. It was private, peaceful, perfect. And when it was finally listed for sale—she refused to consider that it wouldn't eventually be—her piece of heaven would definitely be pricey. And according to Darla, once that prime strip of land was listed, it wouldn't last long. Lexie would need to have enough money ready to act fast.

Speaking of acting fast...Lexie glanced at her trusty waterproof Timex. She was scheduled to accompany a snorkeling group in half an hour. No time for daydreaming if she hoped to grab some much-needed lunch at the outdoor Marine Patio. She finished drying off, slipped on her neon-green T-shirt that read Whispering Palms Activities And Sports Director in bold black letters across the front, the matching shorts, then crammed her wet "pool hair" under her favorite Florida Marlins baseball cap. She was about to reach for her water shoes when she halted, her attention grabbed by a masculine figure standing in the breezeway leading to the lobby. Pushing her Ray•Bans higher on her nose, she peered through the dazzling sunshine, then pursed her lips in involuntary appreciation.

He'd clearly just checked in as he held the colorful trifold pamphlet outlining the resort's amenities and containing the room key-card given to new guests at the reception desk. Decked out in a Stetson hat, long-sleeved shirt, snug jeans, what appeared to be the biggest belt buckle she'd ever seen and cowboy boots, he wasn't dressed for the beach, but even at this distance there was no doubt he filled out those denims *very* nicely.

She squinted at him, but the shade cast by the brim of his hat prevented her from seeing his face. Just then, he turned and headed across the lobby toward the bank of elevators leading to the guest rooms. Hmm. He filled out those jeans as nicely from the back as he had from the front. However, since the temperature hovered somewhere near ninety-five in the shade, hopefully Mr.

Cowboy would change into something cooler before venturing outside.

As she made her way toward the Marine Patio, she couldn't help but wonder what he'd look like out of those jeans.

TWENTY MINUTES LATER she found out.

He looked damned good.

Leaning back in her chair as she washed down the last bite of her tuna salad sandwich with a sip of iced tea, she caught sight of him entering the pool area from the lobby doors. Even though he now wore a bright white T-shirt and a pair of dark blue swim trunks, and the Stetson had been replaced with a baseball cap, there was no mistaking he was the same guy. The way he moved, with that smooth, athletic, confident gait, was a dead giveaway. As was the fine physique.

He appeared to be searching for something or someone as he walked around the pool, weaving his way among the lounging sunbathers.

Stirring her iced tea with her straw, she watched him pause, settling his hands on his hips. With his eyes narrowed against the sun's glare, his gaze slowly panned the pool area. Her own gaze slid over him and again her lips pursed with female appreciation. There was no doubt he fell squarely into the "hunk" category. Tall and broad-shouldered, he had a ruggedly attractive face that looked as if it came straight from one of those tourism print ads for Wyoming or Colorado.

He started walking again, with that slow, measured gait that riveted her attention. Her eyes, which seemed to suddenly develop a mind of their own, zeroed in on the area directly below where his giant belt buckle had been. Pressing her lips together, Lexie swallowed once.

Yup, Mr. Cowboy was definitely put together quite...nicely. In fact, she couldn't recall the last time she'd seen a pair of swim trunks filled out so...perfectly. Maybe he should have stayed covered up in those jeans. No telling what sort of havoc this guy would wreak in those swim trunks.

A sigh of envy escaped her for the woman this hunk was no doubt looking for. Lucky girl. Probably some Pamela Anderson look-alike who favored thong bikinis—and actually looked good in one.

She tried to imagine herself as a Pamela Anderson/thong-sporting/luscious man-magnet and had to force back a laugh.

Not in this lifetime. So engrossed was she in her silly daydream, it took her several seconds to realize that Mr. Cowboy had stopped walking. And that he now stood directly in front of her. And that she was staring at his groin.

A wave of embarrassed heat washed through her and she jerked up her chin, silently thanking the ingenious soul who had invented sunglasses. At least Mr. Cowboy wouldn't know she'd been visualizing his big...belt buckle. Yup, that's what she'd been thinking about. Absolutely. Um, except that he wasn't wearing the belt buckle any longer. But, hey, how would she have known that if she hadn't looked?

Now that her chin was back up where it belonged, she found herself looking at a face that confirmed her earlier assessment of "hunk." He wasn't handsome in the classic sense—his features were too rough, too stark. But there was no denying that the dark brown eyes, the high slash of cheekbones, his firm, full lips and square jaw combined to make an arrestingly attractive face. He looked big and tall, muscular, solid and strong, and even though a small feminist inner voice scolded her for not being immune to his obvious masculinity, everything girly in her heaved out a silent, *Oooohhhhh.*

His gaze settled for a second on her Marlins hat, then tracked slowly downward. She suddenly felt uncharacteristically self-conscious about her pool hair, ratty cap, baggy shorts and damp shirt. Not to mention her suddenly hard nipples—which she longed to blame on a freakish cool breeze, but nothing even remotely resembling a cool breeze had wafted by.

Before she could cross her arms over her chest, he raised his gaze back to hers, then touched the brim of his hat. "You must be Lexie Webster," he said in a deep, sexy voice.

Even if she wasn't Lexie Webster, she suspected no one would have blamed her for claiming she was. Especially since most of the males who sought her out at the resort were normally accompanied by their wives and/or several children. And the rest of them were either under sixteen or over eighty.

Before she could answer he continued, "Tim at the registration desk told me to look for a gal by the pool with a shirt that read Activities And Sports Director." His gaze wandered downward once more, touching on the words emblazoned across her chest, then rose again to meet her eyes. A crooked grin lifted one corner of his mouth and a dimple creased his cheek. "That would appear to be you."

Lexie forced herself not to stare at that dimple, which could be summed up in one word: sexy. Or two words. damn sexy. Offering him a smile she said, "Yes, I'm Lexie Webster. What can I do for you, Mr...?"

He instantly extended his hand. "Maynard. Josh Maynard. I'd like to sign up for your classes."

And wouldn't I love to teach you everything I know. Lexie inwardly scowled at her errant inner voice then shook his hand. A tingle raced up her arm when her palm met his large calloused one in a firm grip. He had a nice handshake. No bone-crushing and no limp, wishy-washy stuff. Releasing his hand she asked, as if she didn't already know and hadn't already ogled him in his cowboy gear, "Are you a guest at the resort, Mr. Maynard?"

"Yes, ma'am. I just checked in, and I'm ready and eager to get started. And please call me Josh."

She couldn't recall the last time someone over the age of twelve had called her "ma'am." "Which classes were you interested in taking, Josh?"

"All of them."

"*All* of them? We offer nearly two dozen." She smiled up at him. "That won't leave you much vacation time for relaxing."

"I'm not here to vacation. I'm here to learn."

"I see." Her lips twitched. "In that case, I'll be sure to sign you up for the Make A Basket From Palm Fronds craft session."

A frown formed between his brows and he settled his hands on his hips, dragging Lexie's gaze involuntarily downward. His long fingers spread out across his hips, pointing like arrows toward his groin. She cleared her throat and instantly jerked her attention upward. Good grief, she was turning into a pervert. Anyone would think she was a sex-starved nympho who'd never seen an attractive, hunky cowboy with a killer dimple.

You are *sex-starved,* her inner voice taunted. *And you never have seen such an attractive, hunky cowboy, let alone one with a killer dimple.*

Hmm. Well, at least she wasn't a nympho. Probably.

And just because it had now been eleven months, three weeks and five days since she'd had sex, that didn't mean she was starved. Heck no. She was merely a bit...peckish. Darla's words flitted through her mind. *You are primed...*

"I reckon the palm frond basket-making is one I can skip," he said, yanking her attention back to the conversation. "What I need to learn is how to sail."

She noted he said *need* as opposed to want. "We offer beginner lessons here at the resort, and I can recommend several excellent sailing schools in the area for more advanced lessons. Do you have any sailing experience?"

"No, ma'am. But I'm a quick learner, and I've read up on the subject. What I need is practical, hands-on instruction." He looked around, as if trying to see if anyone was listening to them. Then he stepped closer, leaning toward her. Warmth that had nothing to do with the bright sun enveloped her, along with his scent—a combination of freshly laundered clothing and some sort of woodsy musk that tapped her hormones on the shoulders and proclaimed, "Boy, does he smell *good.*" She firmly told her hormones to sit down and shut up. Sheesh! She'd taken one look at this guy and lost her marbles. He was probably married with three kids. Or engaged. She glanced down. No ring. But that didn't prove anything.

Lowering his voice he said, "The problem is, Miss Webster—"

"Lexie."

"—yes, ma'am, is that before I learn to sail, I need some more—" he cast another quick look around "—*basic* type of instructions."

"In what area?"

"I'm, uh, well...this is embarrassing to admit, but I'm not a real good swimmer."

Understanding dawned, and sympathy tugged at her. Had he suffered some childhood water-related trauma? Such was often the case when adults couldn't swim. "I see. Well, that's not a problem, Josh, nor should you be embarrassed. I've taught many adults how to swim. We offer classes twice a week—"

"I need more than twice a week, and to be honest, I'd prefer not to take lessons with other folks around—at least not until I develop some proficiency."

"So you want private lessons?"

"Yes, ma'am. I shouldn't need too many. My coordination and strength are good. What I don't have is experience." He laid his hand over his heart and dipped his chin, looking at her with soulful puppy-dog eyes. "Please say you're available to help me. You'd be the answer to my prayers."

Yikes. Was there a woman currently breathing who could resist that look? That heartfelt plea? If so, God bless her.

Lexie quickly mulled over his offer, and just as quickly decided to accept. With the extra cash she could earn teaching Mr. Cowboy, especially now that the tourist season was approaching a lull, he could be the answer to her prayers, as well.

She quoted her hourly rate and he agreed without batting an eye. "When do we start?" he asked, casting an askance glance at the crowded pool.

"The pool is open twenty-four hours, but it's normally unoccupied in the evenings. Why don't we meet here tonight at nine?"

"Nine sounds great. Thank you."

"You're welcome." She glanced down at her watch

and realized her lunch break was over. "I have a snor-keling session now, but I'll see you this evening."

He touched his hat and nodded. "I'm looking for-ward to it, ma'am."

JOSH WATCHED HER zigzag expertly around the lounge chairs on her way toward the beach. His gaze traveled down her back, noting the smooth muscles in her golden-tanned thighs and calves. She was fairly small and compact, but very nicely put together. Between her dark sunglasses and baseball cap, he hadn't been able to see much of her face or hair, but she had a beautiful, friendly smile. And great lips.

A bunch of his buddies were leg men, and some were breast men, some a combination of both, and most pos-sessed an appreciation of the female posterior, as well. While Josh easily admired all those feminine attributes, he was definitely what he'd term a lip man. And Lexie Webster possessed just the sort of well-shaped, full, moist-looking mouth that made him groan.

And by damn, her legs, breasts and posterior were fine-looking, too. And she smelled like one of those long, cool, tropical drinks. The kind that made you want to take a nice big...lick.

To top it all off, he especially liked the fact that she had no idea who he was. Yeah, she'd given him the once-over, but clearly his name and face didn't ring any bells with her, which suited him just fine. A lot of the women who followed the rodeo circuit made big plays for him and, while the attention had been flattering at first, he'd eventually reached the point where he didn't know if a woman liked him for himself or because of his championship titles. He hated to be cynical, but there was no denying that the more competitions he'd won, the more attractive he'd become to the ladies.

But unlike the women from the circuit or from home, Miss Lexie Webster didn't know him from a hole in the ground. And that was perfect. He needed to keep his mind on the task at hand. Learn to swim. Then learn to sail a boat, and then, by damn, sail it, and see something of the world while he did. For himself, and for Dad. After that, he wasn't sure what the future would hold, but for right now, he wasn't looking any further than mastering this water stuff.

Making his way back toward the lobby, he debated the wisdom of hiring an attractive woman to teach him. He recalled the tornado of images that had whirled through his mind when she'd said *So you want private lessons*—images that had nothing to do with swimming or sailing. But he forced the worry aside. He could do anything he set his mind to. He'd just pretend Lexie Webster was one of the guys.

After all, how distracting could one small woman be?

AT EIGHT FORTY-FIVE that evening Josh walked along one of the winding flagstone paths leading toward the pool. Lush vegetation surrounded the meandering walkway. Palms towered overhead, their long curving leaves rustling in the gentle, tropical-scented breeze. A full moon glowed, casting shimmering silver ribbons on the calm ocean, and the soothing splash of one of the grounds' many waterfalls reached his ears.

He nodded to a hand-holding, strolling couple, then, as he crossed over a small wooden bridge, he spied another couple embracing on the beach, backlit by the moon's glow. He could easily see how this setting, with its potent combination of the ocean, the salt air, the swaying palms and the need for very little clothing could turn one's thoughts to romance.

But not him. No sirree. His agenda left no time for canoodling. In fact, romancing of any kind was the furthest thing from his mind. Every last ounce of his concentration was firmly focused on the pool and his upcoming swimming lesson.

He rounded a curve in the path. The pool lay just ahead, its aqua surface glistening under the moonlight, its pale bottom softly lit by underwater lights. During his walk around the grounds after dinner, he'd discovered that this pool was like no other he'd ever seen. It was more part of a series of pools branching off from the main pool, all connected by tunnels. Folks could swim or float in an inner tube from one pool to the next, take a break from the sun in the shade of one of the tunnels, or splash in one of the waterfalls cascading from the rock formations. A swim-up bar was situated along the far side, and steam rose from the trio of hot tubs gurgling from behind another huge rock formation. And here he'd thought pools came in two shapes: rectangle or oval.

A quick glance around indicated the pool area was deserted. Good. His lesson was scheduled to start in about ten minutes, and he didn't relish the thought of an audience gawking at him while he learned something most five-year-olds already knew how to do.

He was just about to drop his towel onto a lounge chair when a splash caught his attention. Turning toward the sound, he froze. And stared.

A feminine figure was emerging from the pool, rising slowly from the shallow end, her curvaceous form revealed inch by tantalizing inch as she seemingly glided toward the wide curved steps leading from the water.

She appeared from that aqua-hued water like a slow-motion shimmering sea nymph, and he suddenly knew how Ulysses must have felt when he caught sight of those sirens.

She climbed the last step, then stood in profile to him at the edge of the pool. Droplets clung to her skin, meandering slowly downward. His gaze followed the path of those drops, and he damn near swallowed his tongue. She had more curves on her than a mountain road. Curves that were put on further heart-stopping display when she stretched, reaching up to smooth her hands over her slicked-back, chin-length hair.

He shook his head to clear away the lustful fog shrouding his brain and also to redirect his eyeballs, which, thank God, were attached to him or they'd have flopped out onto the cement. A frown yanked down his brows, and he huffed out a disgusted sound. What the hell was wrong with him? She was just a gal in a swimsuit. And a plain ol' one-piece swimsuit at that. He'd seen dozens of women today wearing far less. Maybe he could understand him losing his mind like that if this gal'd been wearing a teeny bikini...

Instantly he imagined that curvy form in a teeny bikini, and heat shot through him. He squeezed his eyes shut and pinched the bridge of his nose to dispel the image. Hell, he had to get a hold of himself before his instructor arrived—

"Is that you, Josh?" asked a familiar feminine voice.

He jumped as if he'd squatted on his spurs. Uh-oh. Unless he missed his mark—and he rarely did—that familiar feminine voice came from the exact location where the water nymph stood. And that could only mean one thing.

His swimming instructor, Miss Lexie Webster, was none other than the curvaceous pool goddess.

Forcing his eyes open, he watched her walk toward him. She moved with that same fluid grace he'd noticed this afternoon, only it was easier to see that grace in all its glory now that it wasn't covered up by a baggy T-shirt and shorts.

In spite of the fact that he gave himself a mental kick in the ass and tried to move toward her, he simply stood there as if his feet were glued in place.

When she reached him, she greeted him with a friendly smile. "Ready for your lesson?"

Most likely he nodded, but he wasn't sure. He certainly meant to, but it seemed all he could do was gawk. No doubt about it, he went from zero to smitten in a nanosecond. He'd thought her attractive this afternoon, but now, without the sunglasses and baseball hat, the word that came to mind was...*whew!*

He couldn't tell what color her eyes were in the muted light, but he could tell they were pale. Blue? Green? One or the other. Whatever their color, there was no mistaking how large and expressive they were, or the long, spiky wet lashes surrounding them. His gaze drifted over her pert nose, complete with a dusting of freckles, then settled on her mouth.

The devil himself must have fashioned that wicked mouth because it had sin written all over it. And those two dimples winking on either side of those pouty lips had to be illegal. She stood in front of him, glistening wet, wearing next to nothing...he swallowed in an effort to moisten his dust-dry throat.

"Are you all right, Josh?"

He bobbed his head in a jerky nod.

"Do you still want to take your lesson?"

Lesson? Oh, right. Swimming. He cleared his throat then forced his lips to move. "Yes, ma'am."

"There's no reason to be nervous. I'll be right next to you the entire time." She laid her hand on his arm in what he assumed was meant as a gesture of comfort. Instead it felt as though she'd lit a match to his skin. Had he actually thought he could consider this woman one of the *guys*? Yup, he sure had, which placed him squarely in the category of "a couple steaks short of a barbecue."

A dozen flirtatious responses sprang to his lips, and he clenched his teeth to contain them. This was supposed to be strictly business, but he knew it wouldn't be long before he'd give in to temptation. No way he'd be able to resist flirting with her. Not when she had all his nerve endings on red alert.

"I promise you'll be perfectly safe," she said with a reassuring smile.

He looked into those big eyes of hers and his stomach dropped a good two feet. Somehow he suspected that *safe* was the last thing he would be around this woman.

Reaching out, she grabbed his hand, pulling him gently toward the pool. "C'mon. We'll start nice and slow in the shallow end. You'll be swimming in no time."

Heat from where their palms touched radiated up his arm. *Shallow end, my ass.*

He hadn't so much as dipped his toe in the water, but he had a distinct sinking feeling—which boded particularly bad for the entire swimming scenario—that he was already in way over his head.

2

LEXIE STOOD in the pool, the warm water lapping at her waist, and tried to look busy with her kickboards in an attempt not to watch Josh ready himself for their lesson.

She failed miserably.

The way her eyeballs had annoyingly grown a mind of their own reminded her of those iguanas she'd seen on a recent nature program—their eyes bulged out and worked independently of each other just as hers seemed to be doing now. One eye watched him set his towel on a lounge chair. The other eye ostensibly studied the two kickboards floating next to her.

His hair was dark and thick, her one eye noted. Just the sort of hair that begged for female fingers to ruffle through it. And his legs...whoa, baby. Her earlier assessment was definitely correct: they looked good covered in jeans, they looked incredible *not* covered in jeans. Before she could take that thought and run with it, he grabbed the ends of his gray University of Montana T-shirt and slowly pulled it over his head.

Her kickboard eye nearly swiveled out of its socket to join its mate for an extended ogle as his extremely fine torso and chest was revealed in heart-stopping increments. *Yowza.* Clearly Calvin Klein and Ralph Lauren didn't know about this guy 'cause if they did, Josh Maynard's bod would be featured in every magazine and plastered on billboards and buses across the country. Tight abs, broad shoulders, muscular arms. His wide chest was dusted with dark hair that narrowed down into a dusky ribbon, bisecting his abdomen before disappearing into the waistband of his swim trunks. She instantly imagined tugging on that waistband and playing peekaboo to see where that intriguing path led.

Her gaze dropped several inches and her breath hitched. If *that* was as fine as the rest of him, and she suspected it was, then she'd just ogled one of the finest male specimens she'd ever ogled. And working at the resort, she'd ogled her fair share.

Mr. Cowboy's physique definitely fell into the sigh-inducing category she called "came by it honestly"—from hard work and physical labor—as opposed to the "pretty-boy-perfect" body gained by lifting weights while admiring oneself in the mirror at the local health club.

He neatly folded his shirt, then bent to untie his sneakers. With his attention focused on his shoelaces, she allowed herself a quick peek at his butt. No surprise that his ass was as fine as the rest of him.

Last week's conversation with Darla tickled her memory, and she frowned. Based solely on his looks, Josh Maynard was definitely fling-worthy. But just because the guy's physique hardened her nipples didn't mean he was a good choice. There were a few other things to consider—such as did he harbor homicidal-maniac tendencies?

After setting his Nikes down next to the lounge chair where his shirt and towel rested, he approached the pool. His gaze skimmed intently over the entire surface, as if looking for something. After a moment, apparently satisfied with what he'd seen—or hadn't seen—he appeared to brace himself, then walked down the steps to join her.

"Okay," he said, stopping when several feet separated them. "I'm ready." A crooked grin pulled up one corner of his mouth. "Bring it on."

The moon and the muted overhead lights cast a soft glow over him, accentuating his wide shoulders. Height-wise, he was just right—not too short, not too tall. Her eyes were level with his mouth. His firm, strong, very attractive mouth.

She huffed out a breath. *Good Lord, get a grip on yourself, Lexie. So he's good-looking. So he's built like a god. You don't know anything about him. He probably has five ex-wives. Or five girlfriends. Or is married. Or gay. Or out on parole. And even if he isn't, what difference does it make? He's a transient vacationer. He'll be gone in a week, two weeks tops.*

The third rule of flings suddenly flashed through her mind: temporary.

A transient vacationer certainly met that criteria.

She flexed her fingers, pushing the thought aside—for now. Right now she needed to stop behaving like a hormonal teenager, to act in a professional manner and to get on with the lesson. For the next hour he was a paying customer. She needed the money. Period. After that...well, she'd see how things progressed.

"Tell me, Josh, are you afraid of the water? Have you had a bad experience in the past?"

He hesitated, then said, "I like the water well enough. Pool water, and clear, tropic-type ocean water, that is. The sort where you can see the bottom. But I've never lived near the ocean, and I've rarely had the occasion to use a pool. There's lots of creeks, streams, rivers and watering holes at home, so I had the opportunity but never the...inclination."

"Where is home?"

"Manhattan."

Creeks and watering holes? In *Manhattan*? Who did this guy think he was kidding? He was from Manhattan like she was from the Enchanted Forest. Trying to hide her blank disbelief she said, "You, uh, don't sound like a New Yorker."

"Manhattan, Montana."

"There's a *Manhattan* in Montana?"

"Yes, ma'am. Right in the southwest corner. Proud to call our town The Little Apple, and it's some of the most beautiful land you'd ever want to see. I was born and raised there."

"So are you a cowboy?"

"I am."

"You mean, like a real cowboy? Horses and ranches and cattle and stuff?"

"Yes, ma'am." A slow smile creased his features, coaxing his dimple to appear, while unmistakable mischief danced in his eyes. "Would you like to see my chaps and spurs?"

Would I ever. Heat slivered down her spine and she bit the inside of her cheek. Good grief. If this hunka-hunka gorgeous real cowboy was going to flirt with her, they'd never get this lesson started.

"I'll take your word for it," she said in her most brisk, teacherlike voice. "Now tell me, how much experience do you have in the water?"

His eyes continued to twinkle. "You mean, with regard to swimming?"

The devil inside her actually toyed with the thought of matching his flirtatious demeanor and answering in kind, but she quickly abandoned the idea. She prided herself on her professionalism and commitment to her job. There'd be plenty of time for flirting later—if she decided she actually wanted to indulge.

Shooting him the same warning look and using the same no-nonsense tone she'd perfected on hundreds of adolescent swimming students, she said, "Yes, with regard to swimming."

He sobered, then stroked his chin. "Not much experience, I'm afraid. You see, there was this incident when I was a kid..."

His voice trailed off and sympathy immediately crowded aside any other feelings. Just as she'd suspected. "Did you almost drown?" she asked gently.

"No, ma'am. I was bit."

"Bit?"

"By a snake. We were visiting my uncle in south Texas. I was standing in this creek, in murky water up to about here." He indicated his hips with his hands. "I grabbed for a log floating by, can't think why I did it except it was there. Unfortunately I didn't see the cottonmouth swimming alongside the log, but he saw me. And he let me know it."

"Cottonmouth! They're poisonous!"

"They sure are. Lucky for me, the hospital was close by. Even luckier, the doctor was experienced with snakebites. Turned out the snake had delivered a defensive strike and no venom was injected." A sheepish grin pulled up one corner of his mouth. "I recovered just fine, but I'm afraid that experience sort of soured me toward rivers, lakes, streams and such, so I never learned to swim."

"Perfectly understandable. How old were you?"

"Six. And while I can't say I'd ever want to splash

around in another fresh-water location, I'm fine with the prospect of swimming in a pool or the ocean—as soon as I learn how, that is."

This probably wasn't a good time to inform him that creatures more dangerous than snakes populated the ocean. Instead she said, "I'm so sorry that something so traumatic happened to you."

"Well, thank you. That's certainly nicer to hear than the razzing I'm used to gettin' about it from the boys." He shook his head. "Nuthin' worse than jawing with a bunch of cowboys trading snakebite stories and you having to admit that instead of getting tagged on the boot or the ankle or even the hand, you got bit in the butt. Embarrassing, that's what it is."

She pursed her lips to keep them from twitching at his disgruntled tone. "Look on the bright side," she suggested. "If the snake had been in *front* of you instead of behind you, the entire situation could have been a whole lot worse."

A shudder shook him. "Don't I know it. Can't tell you how many bad moments the mere thought of that scenario inspired."

Hmm. Did he have a cute little scar on his butt? *Wouldn't you like to know,* her inner voice jeered. Lexie mentally thunked herself in the forehead. Good Lord, now she was fantasizing about *scars*. Definitely time to get this lesson started.

Offering him an encouraging smile, she said, "The fact that you're not afraid to be in the pool puts you further along than many people I've taught. One-on-one lessons with an experienced instructor always close by will give you the confidence to overcome your fears. The first thing we need to work on is getting your face in the water and learning to breathe."

He shot her a wink and a smile. "Seeing as how I'm already a first-rate breather, this is fixin' to be easier than I thought."

She firmly ignored the flutter his teasing roused in her. Indicating he should follow, she moved toward the middle of the pool, stopping when the water reached his waist. "I want you to breathe in, then bend forward and put your face in the water. Blow your breath out through your nose, then straighten up." She demonstrated, then asked, "Ready to try?"

"Yes, ma'am." He sucked in a deep breath, then did as she'd instructed. When he rose, a cascade of water ran down his chest and torso. After wiping his eyes, he reached up and tunneled his fingers through his wet hair to push it back from his face. She absolutely did not notice the way his muscles rippled with the movement.

"Any problem doing that?" she asked, forcing her roving eyeballs to remain on his face and not follow the rivulets wandering down his body.

"Nope."

"With many people, getting them to put their face in the water is a major obstacle."

"Doesn't bother me a bit."

"Excellent. Then we can move right on to the next step. Now this time, instead of standing back up to breathe in, I want you to turn your face to the side to breathe. Like this." She performed the movement several times, slowly, noting with satisfaction that he watched her intently. "Make sure you turn your head far enough," she warned. "You don't want to suck in a lungful of water."

They spent the next fifteen minutes working on Josh's technique. He grasped the concept almost immediately, but Lexie had him repeat it over and over.

As with anything else, swimming required practice, and without proper breathing you'd eventually sink like a rock. After a quarter hour she said, "That's great, Josh."

He waggled his brows. "Told you I was a good breather. What's next?"

"Let's see what kind of kicker you are."

He again performed that stretching, push-his-hair-back move while a slow, devastating smile, complete with killer dimple, eased across his wet face. "Bring it on, Miss Lexie."

Her pulse skipped a beat. Yikes. Potent. That's what this guy was. Like a shot of straight brandy. And that smile of his...holy cow. It generated enough heat to fry an egg. Her gaze riveted on his mouth...that lovely, yummy mouth. He was no doubt a great kisser.

Ack! Where had *that* thought come from? Left field somewhere. More like outer space. She shook her head to dislodge the alien who'd clearly taken up residence in her brain. *Swimming. Think swimming. Not kissing. Swimming. As in stroke, stroke, stroke.*

Instantly an image of his big hand stroking her naked body rose in her mind.

Okay, bad analogy.

Pressing her lips together, she moved toward the side of the pool to grab the two kickboards she'd left there, taking those few seconds to give herself another firm and much-needed pep talk. *Get yourself together, you idiot. You're gawking at him like he's a rack of ribs and you're one step away from starvation. You've shared water-related activities with dozens of attractive men. Hell, you almost married one of them. So quit gawking and concentrate on your job.*

Yeah, that's the ticket. Now she felt better. More in

control. While she couldn't deny that this particular guy set all her senses on "tingle," she could ignore that. It wasn't as if swimming was a contact sport. It wasn't as if she had to *touch* him or anything.

Feeling much more in command of herself and her unruly hormones, she handed him one of the kickboards and smiled. "Let's get those legs going."

After showing him how to hold the board, arms extended, they kicked slow, side-by-side laps. After the first few, Lexie showed him how to add his previous lesson by putting his face in the water and turning to breathe. Thirty minutes later she called a halt. Standing in the shallow end, she applauded her pupil.

"Great job, Josh. You'll be swimming like a fish by the end of the week."

He stood, and she silently applauded herself, as well—for keeping her errant eyeballs fixed on his face.

"Well, I really appreciate your help." He walked closer to her, stopping when only two feet separated them. Warmth seemed to radiate off his wet skin...or was that just her skin heating from the inside out? He looked big and solid and wet and delicious. And he was standing *waaaay* too close. "Is that it for tonight?"

She bobbed her head in a jerky nod. "Yes. But I'm very pleased, as you should be. You're a fast learner."

"You're a good teacher." He tunneled his fingers through his wet hair, and she bit down on the tip of her tongue to keep it from flopping out of her suddenly dry mouth at the rippling of all those lovely muscles. "When's our next lesson? How about early tomorrow morning?"

He certainly was eager to learn. "I'm afraid I'm already booked in the kid's camp for the two hours before my normal shift begins. What about tomorrow night at nine?"

"Tomorrow is Friday."

"Yes. Do you have other plans?"

"No." His gaze flickered downward and rested on her mouth for several seconds. That brief glance touched her like a heated caress, sending her pulse into double time. "I'm just surprised that *you* don't." He raised his gaze back to hers. "Tomorrow is fine with me. What's on the agenda for the next lesson?"

Lexie swallowed and fought the sudden urge to wipe her overheated brow. When the heck had the temperature risen to three hundred degrees? "Ah, I'll teach you how to float..." Her eyes widened and she gulped. Uh-oh. Floating involved touching. Lots of touching. His gorgeous, nearly naked body.

"You okay?"

No. I feel like I just backed into a furnace. "I'm fine. We'll be covering, um, floating, then I'll teach you some basic strokes."

Something heated and intense flared in his eyes and his gaze again dropped to her lips. Good grief, if he didn't stop looking at her like that, she was going to do something that would no doubt mortify her for the rest of her natural days. Such as blurt out a barrage of questions similar to, "Are you married or otherwise unavailable? Are you as attracted to me as I am to you? Does your mouth taste as good as it looks?"

Reaching out, he touched a single, wet fingertip to her shoulder, then slowly dragged it down her arm. Goose bumps beaded her flesh, completely at odds with the inferno his feather-soft touch ignited.

"Teach me some basic strokes," he murmured in a

husky voice that tripled her pulse rate. "That sounds very...educational. I'm looking forward to it."

Without another word he nodded to her, then exited the pool. She tried to keep her eyeballs from staring at him, but her brain apparently wasn't capable of sending out the proper signals. Damn it, the man had barely touched her, yet he'd fried her circuits but good.

Her circuits took another jolt when he crouched to pick up his belongings. Holy cow. Those wet swim trunks clung to his backside in an exceptionally fine way. Hmm. Exactly where might that snakebite scar be, assuming he had one?

No sooner had that thought registered in her befuddled mind than he turned to face her. Holy double cow. Those wet swim trunks clung to his front side in an absolutely heart-stopping way. He blew that entire "cold water causes penis shrinkage" theory literally out of the water.

He draped his towel over his shoulders, then nodded at her. "Till tomorrow." Before she could reply—which could well have taken a week since she'd apparently forgotten how to speak—he headed down the darkened path and, within seconds, disappeared from sight.

Lexie blew out a deep breath. Walking to the edge of the pool, she hoisted herself onto the edge. She wrapped her towel around her, then pulled her cell phone from her gym bag. A quick glance at her waterproof watch showed it was ten o'clock. Sort of late for a weeknight, but Darla would understand. This was an emergency.

An image of Josh Maynard's wet body flashed in her mind and she hastily punched in Darla's number.

No doubt about it, this was a full-scale, five-alarm emergency. The instant Darla answered, Lexie said, "I think I've found my fling guy."

3

"Oh, he definitely sounds like your fling guy," Darla said half an hour later over drinks at Mermaid's, a local bar. "You need to have sex with him. As soon as possible."

Lexie nearly spewed out a mouthful of margarita. Good grief, Darla certainly didn't mince words. Lexie managed to swallow, but the frozen drink went down the proverbial wrong pipe, starting up a coughing fit. While she gasped and sputtered, Darla calmly waggled two fingers at their waiter, indicating they wanted another round.

"Do I need to Heimlich you?" Darla asked, dragging a tortilla chip through the queso dip then popping the morsel into her mouth.

Lexie shook her head, coughed a few more times, then took a deep breath. Recovered, she glared across the table. "No, the Heimlich isn't necessary. But—"

Darla cut off her words by raising her perfectly manicured hand in a stop motion. "Let me guess," Darla said. "You agreed you need a fling. You *want* to have a fling. But now that there's actually a potential fling-worthy guy on your radar screen, you're nervous."

Lexie could only stare. "What are you, psychic?"

"No. Just been there, done that enough times to recognize the symptoms. You're wondering if your reaction to him was just some sort of hormonal aberration, and you're trying to mentally compile a list of reasons why you shouldn't have anything to do with him."

"Impressive. Do you tell fortunes, also?"

Darla dipped another chip and waggled her elegant brows. "Yup. I see lots of sex in your immediate future."

The mere thought crept warmth up Lexie's neck. "But what about those dozen reasons I came up with why I shouldn't have anything to do with him?"

"You came up with a dozen reasons why you shouldn't have sex with a man who makes you sweat in a *pool*? You're kidding. I can't think of *one*. You experienced a perfectly normal, healthy, physical reaction to an attractive man, and it's about damn time. So what's the problem?"

"For starters, I don't know anything about him. Like his marital status and if he's out on parole for being an ax murderer."

Darla waved a dismissive hand. "That can be remedied by asking a few questions. What else?"

Lexie hesitated. "It's sort of difficult to explain. I guess I'm surprised by my strong reaction to him. I'm surrounded by attractive men all the time, but I don't want to remove their clothes with my teeth."

"That's because you're honorable, and until about eleven months ago you were engaged to Tony. This is a simple matter of logic. You haven't had a man in almost a year. Good Lord, Lexie, that's just not natural. Your body's had enough of celibacy." She pointed a tortilla chip at Lexie. "If you were thirsty, what would you do?"

"Have a drink."

"And if you're hungry?"

"Eat."

Darla leaned back in the vinyl-upholstered booth with a triumphant smile. "Exactly. Your body knows what it wants. What it needs. And what it needs is a good sweaty bout of stress-relieving sex. And it wants that sweaty bout of sex with that gorgeous cowboy. From what you've told me about him, he sounds fun and wild, and he's certainly temporary—all the rules for a fling."

"I know. Yet as incredibly tempting as a bout of sweaty sex sounds, I'm hesitant. How can I have sex with a stranger? For all I know, he's some sort of wacko."

"And for all you know, he's a sweetheart. You're not looking to *marry* him. Think of him as your 'transitional' man. You've been out of the social scene for a long while. You need someone temporary to ease you back in. Get you back in the saddle, so to speak. And a cowboy who ignites you like a blowtorch is just the man for the job." Darla leaned forward again, resting her elbows on the scarred wooden tabletop. "Look. You've mourned over your breakup with Tony long enough—"

"I have not been mourning. I've been busy. There's a difference." Lexie twirled her straw in the remnants of her drink. "You know I don't regret ending things with Tony. He was a good guy—at least until I lost him to the glamorous world of extreme sports—but I just couldn't live like that anymore. Never knowing if he was going to come home in one piece, spending half my time at the hospital." She dragged her hands down her face. "You know you're at the hospital too much when you're on a first-name basis with all the emergency room nurses. Give me a nice safe accountant. An insurance guy. Banker. Chef. Gardener. But no more daredevils. You're supposed to grow old *with* someone—not *because* of them. I can't go through that again."

"You'd be insane to even consider it," Darla agreed as their waiter deposited two more margaritas in front of them, then left them alone once more. "Any idea what Tony's up to?"

"Nope. I assume he's on his Everest expedition. After that he planned to run the Amazon on a raft." She shot Darla a rueful smile. "I wouldn't be surprised if after the Amazon he decided to kayak over Niagara Falls."

A visible shudder shivered through Darla. "He was insane, Lexie. He had absolutely no fear. Skydiving, bungee jumping, rock climbing...it just wasn't right. And let's face it, after he won that skydiving competition, after almost dying in the attempt, he turned into a—"

"Jerk. I know." Lexie blew out a sigh. "You would think that a close brush with death would have made him less inclined to risk himself, but instead it pushed him the other way. Made him take *more* risks, seek out higher levels of danger. Like he had something to prove."

"Mmm-hmm. And he sure didn't seem to mind all the adoration from those assorted blondes, brunettes, and redheads who came along with that extreme sport lifestyle. Guess he felt he had something to prove in that area, as well."

"His womanizing definitely was the final nail in the coffin," Lexie agreed.

"I have to say, you took the whole thing pretty calmly, Lex. I would have damaged the guy."

"I wasn't calm at all. I was hurt and angry, but honestly more sad than anything. Sad for him that nearly losing his life set him on such a self-destructive course.

Sad for both of us that his success so drastically changed the sweet guy I fell in love with into someone I couldn't live with."

A determined look entered Darla's eyes. "Well, it's over between you, and now, finally, you've met a man who rings your bell. If you're worried about not knowing him, then get to know him a bit first. How long is he staying at the resort?" She shot Lexie a knowing look. "You did check, didn't you?"

A guilty flush heated her skin. "Yeah, I checked. He's registered for the next three weeks."

Darla raised her brows. "Seems to me you could find out a whole bunch about a man in a lot less time than that. In fact, I'd say a clever girl could find out everything she needed to know over a few drinks."

"He hasn't asked me to go for drinks."

"Have you lost your voice? Ask him. Invite *him* to join you for a beer after your lesson tomorrow night." She waved her hand around, encompassing their noisy surroundings. "Bring him here to Mermaid's. It's cozy and fun. Or how about the bar at the resort? Ply him with liquor, ask him probing, personal questions until you know him better, then have your wicked way with him." She waggled her brows. "Find out if that snake left a scar."

Lexie sighed. "I cannot believe I'd ever want to see another scar. Tony had more of the darn things than Florida has sand fleas. What's *wrong* with me?"

"Nothing. You're in lust. It's normal. Accept it, and act on it. You need to do this. You need to stop working nonstop and enjoy yourself. You're young, attractive, unattached, primed for action and suffering from a crisis-level lack of sex. The timing is perfect. I mean, when were you planning to have a fling? When you're a grandma? *Ask him out.*"

"What if he isn't interested?"

"Then he's an idiot and you're better off without him. Did he seem uninterested during your lesson?"

Lexie recalled how he'd looked at her, with all that focused attention, then how he'd trailed his finger down her arm. "No, but—'

"Lex, the worst that will happen is that you'll go for drinks and he'll turn out to be a dunce, in which case you won't find him attractive anymore. Best case is that he'll prove charming and nice and irresistible, and you'll have yourself a fun fling for a few weeks." Darla reached out and squeezed Lexie's hands. "It's a win-win situation."

Lexie chewed on her bottom lip and pondered Darla's advice. Josh Maynard had struck a chord in her that hadn't been strummed in a long time. Her self-confidence had definitely taken a wallop from her breakup with Tony, whose growing preference for daredevil escapades over her—not to mention his sudden fondness for being surrounded by hordes of admiring women—had eventually left her feeling unneeded, unwanted and unattractive. Josh was the first guy who'd aroused her flattened libido since. And the beauty of a vacation fling was that in three weeks, Josh would be gone. No running into him around town, no awkward meeting up at local parties. *Fun, wild and temporary.*

So what harm could there be in inviting him for a drink? It was as good a way as any to find out if he was as attractive as he seemed. Maybe after some conversation she'd decide he wasn't all that great. Or maybe she'd decide he was fling-worthy. One thing was for certain: if she didn't try, she'd never know. And she definitely wanted to know.

"Okay," Lexie said. "I'll ask him out for a drink."

"Good girl," Darla said, beaming her approval. "So what's this hunk's name?"

"Josh Maynard. Even sounds cowboyish."

Darla frowned. "And vaguely familiar." She pursed her lips, then shrugged. "But it can't be. I don't know a soul from Montana. In fact, I've never met a real, live cowboy."

"Me, either." A laugh escaped her. "But it seems like a tame enough occupation. I mean, what do they do around a ranch? Ride horses and check fences? At least he's not a wild daredevil like Tony."

Darla laughed with her. "Really. The worst thing that could happen to Mr. Cowboy is getting saddle sore."

"Hmm. Could be a good excuse to offer him a massage."

A giggle erupted from Darla. "Yee-ha. Now you're talkin', pardner."

WHEN JOSH ARRIVED at the pool the following evening, the first thing he saw was her...the water nymph who had drifted through his nighttime dreams then occupied his thoughts all day long. She cut through the aqua water with strong, clean strokes, then executed an underwater flip turn before starting the next lap. She completed six more pool lengths before she stopped, hoisting herself to the edge while water cascaded down her curvy form.

Another simple, one-piece, no-nonsense swimsuit hugged her body, and Josh smothered a rueful grimace at his swift physical reaction. No doubt about it, she attracted him like a fly to a bug zapper. His inner voice tried to remind him how those poor flies ended up, but he swatted the warning away.

She caught sight of him and stilled. For several heart-beats they simply looked at each other. His pulse seemed to stall, then thump like a bass drum. She licked her lips, a gesture that forced him to swallow a groan, then offered him a smile. "Hi, Josh. How are you?"

Hot and bothered and it's all your fault. Damn, he didn't know if he wanted her to put some clothes on or to take that bathing suit off. Well, he knew which one he *wanted*...but that didn't mean that it was the smartest. "I'm fine, Lexie. How about you?"

"I'm terrific."

You sure are. He didn't know how many laps she'd swum before he'd arrived, but she wasn't even winded. Water glistened on her well-toned arms and legs, and his already drumming pulse quickened. There was nothing more attractive to him than a physically fit, ath-letic woman, and this particular woman was...whew. Just right.

"I saw you practicing with the kickboard this morn-ing," she said. "I was impressed—not only by your improvement, but by your dedication. It was barely 7:00 a.m."

"I'm determined to master swimming as quickly as possible. And once I set my mind to something...well, as we cowboys say, if you're gonna go, go like hell."

"In that case, ready to get started?"

"Yes, ma'am. I place myself in your hands."

He fancied that something flashed in her eyes, but it disappeared before he could decide. Jerking her head in a nod, she turned then walked down the steps into the water. He followed, relieved when the cool water took the edge off his budding ardor.

"Except for your early morning practicing, I didn't see you around today," she remarked once they stood waist-deep. A teasing glint entered her eyes. "We missed you at Make A Basket From Pond Fronds."

He laughed. "I arranged for a rental car, then spent the day visiting marinas to check out sailboats."

"Did you see anything you liked?"

Sure did. And she's smilin' at me right now. "Lots of nice boats, but before I buy one, I want to know how to sail. And before I can tackle that, I need to learn to swim."

"Have you made reservations for the beginner sailing course offered at the resort?"

"Not yet. Are you the teacher?"

"Yes." She shot him a grin. "Don't worry. I'm fully certified."

"Why do you only offer beginner lessons?"

"It's really all that's necessary here at the resort. If a guest wants more in-depth instructions, we make arrangements for them to attend a sailing school in the area. Or, if a guest prefers, they can hire a staff member for private instructions during off-hours."

"Like I hired you for swimming lessons."

"Exactly."

"Are you available for private sailing lessons?"

"Yes, but only early in the morning, weather permitting, before my normal shift starts. For obvious safety reasons, I don't teach sailing at night." She cocked her head to one side. "Let me know if you're interested."

Oh, I'm interested all right. More interested than a hungry hound dog in a pork chop. And he couldn't deny it irked him. Falling in lust had not been on his list of things to do while in Florida. Still, as that was the hand he'd been dealt, and it had taken him all of one restless night and day to realize he couldn't talk himself out of this attraction, he'd simply have to put up his ante, so to speak, and play—keeping his cards close to the vest, of course.

"Before we begin anything new," she said, "let's spend a few minutes warming up by reviewing what we did last evening." He agreed, then spent the next quarter hour kicking along with the board and breathing.

"Great job, Josh," she said. "You're ready to graduate to floating."

Josh watched her demonstrate lying on her back, as if she were stretched out in a comfortable bed, her arms moving gently back and forth. She closed her eyes and looked for all the world as if she were taking a nap. Sort of like a wet, floating Sleeping Beauty. Her short, dark hair surrounded her head like an undulating halo, and he barely resisted the urge to sift his fingers through the tempting strands. His gaze rested on her full lips and his imagination immediately ran amok, casting him in the role of Prince Charming. Would those gorgeous lips taste as delicious as they looked?

"The keys are relaxation and balance," she said in a soft, soothing voice that thankfully yanked him back to reality. She floated with seemingly effortless grace. "You'll be right next to the edge, so if you feel yourself tipping, just reach out your hand. Like this." She reached out, but instead of touching the edge of the pool, her fingers slid across his belly.

He hissed in a breath and her eyes popped open, clearly realizing she'd made contact with him, not the concrete edge. With a splash, she stood, and emitted a shaky-sounding laugh. "Sorry about that."

"No problem." Nope, none at all. Except that that single inadvertent brush of her hand made him feel as if a firecracker sizzled in his swim trunks. He dragged his hands through his wet hair. Maybe he should have taken these swim lessons in Antarctica. With a male instructor.

"Once you get the hang of this in the pool," she said, "it will be even easier in the ocean where the saltwater has more buoyancy. Unless, of course, the water is rough, but the forecast is calling for calm seas for the next few days. Lots of sunshine and little wind. Not great for sailing, but perfect for swimming. Now, just lie on your back and let the water support you. I'll help you get started."

Josh did as she bid, and was doing a darn good job of it. Or at least he was until she "helped him get started." He'd gotten himself almost supine when she slid her hands under him, one supporting his shoulders, the other the small of his back.

"Good. Now just relax, Josh," she said in a soft, smoky voice.

Relax? With her hands on him, feeling like liquid silk against his skin? With his face not six inches from her full breasts? With her looking at him with those wide, incredible eyes? Not much chance of that.

To his embarrassment, he started floundering like a fish on a hook, his arms and legs flailing. Certainly no one who saw him now would ever believe that he possessed an innate, nearly flawless sense of balance that had enabled him to win four consecutive world rodeo championships.

"Take it easy," she said. "Close your eyes and take slow, deep breaths. Hold on to the side with one hand and let yourself go limp. I've got you."

Limp. Yeah, right. Definitely not much chance of *that*. He snapped his eyes shut, grabbed the concrete edge of the pool, and forced himself to relax, one tense muscle at a time—a feat much easier to accomplish now that he wasn't looking at her, and easier still once he pretended she was an old man. With one tooth. And a grizzled beard.

But then her velvety-soft voice flowed over him once more. "Much better, Josh."

His eyes popped open and he found himself staring up into her lovely face, which hovered so tantalizingly close…so close he had only to reach up to tangle his fingers in her wet hair and pull her mouth down to his…

The flailing and splashing started all over again. If she'd let go of him, he'd have sunk like a millstone, arms and legs waving like a flag in a gale storm. Of course, if she hadn't been holding him, touching him in the first place, he wouldn't have been flopping around in such an undignified way. Damn it, it was downright humiliating that he couldn't master such a simple task. Not to mention aggravating. It left him feeling vulnerable in a way he couldn't recall ever before experiencing. Gritting his teeth, he squeezed his eyes shut once again, pulled together all his concentration, and forced himself to relax.

"Good," she said. "Now, I'm going to move, to stand behind you, by your head, and support your shoulders. Don't worry about sinking below the surface. I promise I won't let you. What I want you to do is to move your arms and legs slowly in the water, like you're making a snow angel. I bet you made a lot of those in Montana."

He kept his eyes firmly closed. "Sure did."

"Then you'll be an expert floater in no time. Just pretend you're lying in a pile of snow. Remember, relax, and balance. You don't have to let go of the side until you feel ready. There's no rush. I'm going to move now, so start making that angel."

Her arm slipped from beneath the small of his back. Focusing on the task for all he was worth, he followed her instructions, conjuring up a mental image of himself as a child, tossing his body into a snowdrift with youthful abandon to create white, frosty angels. *That's it, old boy. Think snow. Ice. Relax and balance.* As long as he kept his mind on the task at hand instead of on her, he'd be fine.

He moved his limbs slowly back and forth in the water, and the more he felt the tension ease from his shoulders, the more buoyant he became. Still, he'd best not relinquish his hold on the side yet.

"Tell me about your home, Josh," he heard her say, though she sounded muffled as his ears were under water. "What's it like in Manhattan, Montana?"

He grasped the opportunity to keep his thoughts away from her like a drowning man seizes a life ring, although he wryly admitted to himself that that was not a good analogy under the present circumstances.

"Manhattan is beautiful. Peaceful." One corner of his mouth quirked upward. "They don't call Montana 'Big Sky Country' for nothing. The sky is so blue it can make your eyes hurt to look at it. The air is crisp and clean, and the mountains look close enough to reach out and touch. Manhattan's rural, lots of wide-open spaces, but the town itself has everything anyone could need— movie theater, restaurants, lots of businesses and shops and such."

"Do you live on a ranch?"

"I do. On a small spread my dad and I bought together last year. Before that I lived and worked at the Dry Creek Ranch where Dad was foreman."

"Does he still work there?"

The familiar grief rolled through him, tightening his throat. "No. He died. Six months ago. On the job. Heart attack."

He felt her fingers flex on his shoulders blades. "I'm so sorry."

A long breath eased from his lips. "Me, too. My dad was a great guy. Patient, kind, always had a friendly word for everyone, no matter how ornery they might be. And I've never met anyone who could handle animals the way he could. He had a true gift."

His dad's weatherbeaten features, blue eyes crinkling at the corners, rose in his mind's eye. He could almost hear Dad's husky-timbred voice say, *Let go of the edge now, son. A man can't succeed if he doesn't try, and if he's gonna try, he's gotta try his best.*

Slowly, one finger at a time, Josh let go of the edge. He felt himself dip lower in the water, but true to her promise, Lexie didn't let him sink below the surface. *Balance and relax.* He gently swished both arms through the water, delight and surprise filling him when he actually remained afloat.

"What about the rest of your family?" came her next muffled question.

"Don't have much, except my uncle and two cousins in Texas. We only see each other maybe once a year, if that. No brothers or sisters, and my mom passed away when I was twelve. After she died, Dad and I moved out to Dry Creek Ranch."

"Your dad never remarried?"

"No. Over the years there were a few ladies whose company he enjoyed, and Lord knows, plenty of women batted their eyes in his direction, but he died loving my mother. They were high school sweethearts.

They'd been married fifteen years when she died, but they'd still acted like kids on a date. Huggin' and kissin' and holding hands."

He thought he heard her blow out one of those feminine, dreamy sighs. "That's lovely. Romantic. And sad. And...lovely."

"Yeah. They were great together. And she sure was a great mom. I remember coming home from school, doing my homework at the kitchen table. Mom would chat with me while she rolled out dough for another loaf of bread she would either burn or undercook." A chuckle worked its way up his throat. "Man, oh, man, she made the worst bread in the world, but she was determined. Can't tell you how many loaves Dad and I slathered butter on and bravely ate because she'd tried so hard. She had a beautiful smile. It lit up her whole face. I remember she smelled like chocolate-chip cookies. She baked them for me every Monday. She burned those a lot, too, but I ate them anyway. They're still my favorite..."

His voice trailed off as a barrage of memories assaulted him...of himself, after his mother's death, angry at the world and the insidious cancer that had taken her so cruelly and quickly, leaving a yawning hole in his heart where her love and laughter and smiles had always dwelt.

And of Dad, so heartbroken that Josh feared he'd lose him, too. The man didn't eat, didn't sleep. Six months after his mother died, he woke up in the middle of the night and found Dad sitting in Mom's favorite easy chair. Tears streamed silently down Bill Maynard's face as he clutched his dead wife's favorite flannel shirt to his chest. It was threadbare at the elbows and faded from hundreds of washings. It used to be Dad's shirt,

but he'd loaned it to her on their first date to a high
school football game, and the shirt, along with Dad,
had been hers from that day forward.

He'd looked at his father, his tears falling onto that
soft cotton, and all the grief he'd stored inside came
pouring out like a burst dam. They'd spent the rest of
the night talking. About her. About the million things
they loved about her. As dawn broke, they agreed that
living in their small house, where she permeated every
corner of every room, was too painful. She'd made the
cozy space into a place filled with love, but it wasn't
home without her. Better to keep it a happy home and
let another family enjoy it. They sold it to a young couple with a baby on the way, then moved out to the Dry
Creek, their memories of Maggie Maynard stored in
boxes and embedded in their hearts. It had taken them
a while to find their footing again, but they'd eventually succeeded.

His thoughts returned to the present, and he became
aware of the silence. Damn, how long had he been lost
in the past? He'd certainly dropped the conversational
ball. Lexie probably thought he was an idiot. Opening
his eyes, he scanned around him.

He was alone. Floating in the middle of the pool, bob-
bing on the surface like a cork.

From the corner of his eye he saw Lexie, leaning
against the edge, grinning and giving him a thumbs-
up.

He only took in half a swallow of chlorinated water
while ungracefully setting his feet back on the bottom.
Standing, with the water lapping at his chest, he
grinned back at her. "Looks like I'm gettin' the hang of
it."

"Indeed you are," she agreed. "Before you know it,

you'll be ready for the Olympic floating team. I'm proud of you."

"Thanks. But I was flappin' around like a broken windmill till you got me talking about home." No need to tell her that his flappin' was all *her* fault.

She smiled. "I've found that directing a student's thoughts away from the water, toward something comfortable and familiar, often does the trick."

"Hope I didn't gab your ears off."

She tugged on her lobes. "Nope. Still attached." Her gaze shifted briefly to her sports watch. "I'm afraid our time's up for tonight."

His attention riveted on the trails of water wandering down her arm, and all thoughts of swimming instantly evaporated from his mind. He walked slowly toward her, enjoying the way her eyes widened at his approach, especially enjoying the way her tongue peeked out to moisten her full lips. He stopped when only two feet separated them.

"I'm disappointed our lesson is over. As I recall, you're next going to teach me some...basic strokes."

Their gazes fused, and his heart performed a slow roll. The way she was looking at him...not with the blatant invitation he often read in women's eyes, but with a combination of unmistakable interest mixed with a hint of uncertainty...

Whew. If she could heat his blood with a mere innocent look, what the hell would happen if he touched her? Gave in to his gnawing craving and kissed her?

He didn't know, but by damn, he was determined to find out.

Right now.

4

LEXIE STOOD FROZEN in place, heart pounding, the rough concrete of the pool apron abrading her shoulders, her mind a blank except for the mantra pumping through it. *He's going to kiss me. He's going to kiss me.*

She'd thought about little else during their lesson. She'd watched him as he'd floated, his eyes closed, staring at his sexy mouth form words about his home. Imagining that sexy mouth on hers.

Bracing his hands against the edge on either side of her, he bracketed her between his strong arms. His gaze slid from her eyes down to her mouth, and he leaned slowly forward. A brushfire of heat sizzled through her.

His lips brushed softly over hers, once, twice, with a teasing gentleness that immediately made her want more. Parting her lips, she touched her tongue to his bottom lip. And in a heartbeat the kiss changed from gentle to Oh. My. God.

With a low groan, he stepped closer. His arms came around her, his mouth covered hers. She was completely surrounded by him. By the delicious feel of his body pressing against hers. The warmth emanating from his wet skin. His large hands combing through her hair then skimming slowly down her back. The exquisite sensation of his tongue exploring her mouth.

Wrapping her arms around his waist, she indulged

herself in the onslaught of sensations assaulting her. Everything faded except the need to feel more of him. Taste more him. Touch more of him. She ran her palms up his back, reveling in the contrast of textures of smooth, firm skin over hard muscle. Desire, hot and insistent and for so long forgotten, gushed through her, turning her insides to syrup. His hands slipped down to the small of her back and puller her closer. His erection pressed against her belly, inspiring a dizzying myriad of sensual images of him, and her, together.

A shriek of feminine laughter broke through the fog of arousal engulfing her. Clearly Josh heard it, too, because he lifted his head. A long mental *nooooooo* of protest echoed in Lexie's lust-frazzled brain at the abrupt end to their kiss, and she forced her eyes open. Josh stared at her with an expression that seemed to simultaneously say "I want more" and "What the hell just happened?" The perfect mirror of her own thoughts.

Another burst of giggles sounded and Lexie turned toward the noise. A young couple emerged from the pathway leading from the beach. Arms entwined, laughing, they skirted the perimeter of the pool, so wrapped up in each other they never even noticed Lexie and Josh.

Pulling in a much-needed deep breath, Lexie returned her attention to Josh and found him still studying her with enough simmering heat to melt a polar ice cap, heat made all the more intense by the fact that their bodies still touched from chest to knee.

The need to say something, to break the tension-fraught silence, pushed at her, but unfortunately the only words that came immediately to mind were "Wanna get naked, cowboy?" Since that seemed somewhat lacking in finesse, she remained silent.

Finally he spoke. "That was some kiss."

She swallowed to locate her voice. "Can't argue with you on that."

The dimple in his cheek flashed. "Now that's a trait I really like in a woman."

"Being a good kisser?"

"Well, yeah, but I meant not arguing with me. And besides, you're not a good kisser."

"Oh?" She deliberately shifted her gaze down to where his erection still pressed against her, then looked back up at him with raised brows. "This..." she drawled, giving him a gentle nudge with her pelvis, "tells me differently."

"It sure does. It means you're an *incredible* kisser."

His words, delivered in that aroused-husky voice, combined with the desire so obvious in his eyes, was like a balm to her bruised feminine ego. His gaze slid down to her mouth, making it clear he intended to kiss her again. Her heart stuttered at the thought, but common sense prevailed and she laid her hands on his chest.

"Not a good idea, Josh."

He stilled, his gaze questioning. "Because...?"

"While there's no sense in pretending that that kiss wasn't mind-blowing, this isn't an appropriate place, especially for me." She dropped her voice to a conspiratorial whisper. "The resort sort of frowns on its employees engaging in passionate exchanges in the pool."

"That's understandable. Disappointing, but understandable."

Resuming her normal voice, she said, "You're paying me for swimming lessons. Let's keep it to just that while we're in the pool."

He nodded slowly. "All right. But what about once we're out of the pool?"

A quick war waged inside her—the part that wanted to remain in her safe cave versus the woman that wanted, needed, to break free. Break-free woman won, hands down. "Why don't we get dressed, then meet in the hotel bar? We can have a drink and some conversation and...see what happens."

His gaze remained steady on hers, and she could almost hear him reflecting her own thought. *I think we both know what's going to happen.*

"All right," he said.

"Great." He didn't move, and after a few seconds she said, "If you'll just back up, I'll—"

"I can't do that."

"Sure you can."

"No, I can't."

"Why not?"

"Because you're standing on my foot."

She looked down and, sure enough, the underwater lights showed that she was indeed standing on his foot. Good grief, he even had good-looking feet. Good-looking, *big* feet. Darla's smirk rose in her mind's eye. *You know what they say about men with big feet, Lexie.*

Yup, she knew. And the impressive size of his erection pressing against her left no doubt that the saying was true in Josh's case. The mere thought fired up a sizzle of lust that all but crispy-fried her synapses. Definitely time to get out of the water before she did something in a public place that could lead to an arrest.

She slid her foot from his, then waded purposefully toward the steps. Exiting the warm water, she wrapped her towel around her body, feeling the need to put something between her and this unsettling man who had all but turned her into one big, pulsating hormone. Jeez, her reaction to him bordered on embarrassing. Surely she'd be able to remain more focused, be more able to think and to carry on a conversation, once they were both dressed and there was a table, a couple of beer mugs, and maybe an order of wings between them.

When she turned around, she noted with relief that he'd exited the pool and slipped on his T-shirt. Grabbing up her things, she said, "I'll head over to the employees' locker room to change. See you in the bar in thirty minutes?"

"Wouldn't miss it." His dimple winked at her, and she had to force herself not to lick her lips. Lips that still tingled from the feel of his. But there was no stopping the *yum, yum* that wafted through her mind.

SITTING IN A CORNER booth, Josh watched Lexie walk into the bar and every one of his nerve endings jumped like a bronc coming out of the chute. She wore a black tank top, a full, fire-engine-red skirt whose hem skimmed her toned legs at mid-thigh, and low-heeled black sandals. Her shiny dark hair curled around her head like a halo. She looked fresh, clean and damn near good enough to eat. And God knows he'd been ready to devour her in the pool. The instant she'd touched her tongue to his lip, she'd set him off like a bottle rocket. He couldn't recall the last time he'd felt such intense, instantaneous combustion. Sure, he'd experienced sparks plenty of times before, but nothing like *that*.

If she hadn't called a halt, he didn't doubt for a second that things in the pool would have quickly burned out of control. This was better, his mind told his protesting body for the dozenth time since he'd exited the pool. Based on her suggestion to meet for drinks and conversation, he clearly sensed that she wanted them to spend some time getting to know each other a bit before they explored where that kiss would lead. Well, that was fine with him. He was definitely interested in finding out more about her, and more than willing to give the lady whatever she wanted and needed.

The lady in question grinned and waved at the bartender, holding up two fingers at him. Then her gaze panned the room. As the bar was half-empty, she spotted him almost immediately, and made her way across the polished wood floor to his table.

Sliding across from him into the booth, she smiled and said, "Hi."

A cloud of some incredible, sexy, flowery fragrance wafted over him, fogging his brain. Thirty minutes. How the hell had she gone from soaking-wet swim teacher to this curly haired, scrumptious-smelling siren in thirty minutes? Good Lord, he knew women who took longer than that just to apply their makeup. He narrowed his eyes at her. It didn't appear she was wearing any makeup, and if she was, it wasn't much. In fact, all he could detect for sure was a hint of gloss on her lips that made them look even more tempting than usual.

Forcing his gaze away from that enticing mouth, their eyes met, and for the first time he could clearly see their color. Hazel. An intriguing mix of amber flecks on a bluish-gray background.

She waved her hand in front of his face, breaking him out of his stupor. "You okay, Josh?"

Nope. Feel like I've just been tossed from the saddle. Recalling that this was supposed to be a conversation/

get-to-know-each-other session, he returned her smile. "Yup, just fine. You fix up real nice, Miss Lexie."

"Ha. You're only saying that because this is the first time you've seen me when I haven't looked like someone just dumped a bucket of water over my head."

Before he could assure her that she looked just fine all wet, a pretty redheaded waitress delivered two frosty mugs of beer to the table. "Hey, Lexie," she said with a smile, then she gave him a friendly nod. "Can I bring you two anything to eat?"

Lexie looked at him. "Hungry?"

"Always."

A flicker of awareness glimmered in her eyes. "Any preferences?"

"Anything you choose will be just fine with me."

"Hmm. Any aversion to spicy food?"

"The spicier the better."

"You're not a vegetarian, are you?"

"You're askin' a *cowboy* that?"

"Right. Dumb question." Turning toward the waitress, she said, "We'll have the extra-large Five-Alarm Platter, Lisa."

"Comin' right up," Lisa said with a jaunty smile, then she turned and headed back toward the bar.

"What's in this Five-Alarm Platter?" he asked, leaning forward to rest his forearms on the table, bringing him closer to her.

"Wings, chili fries, short ribs, quesadillas and cheese-stuffed jalapeños. All spiced up enough to make you breathe fire. Definitely not for the fainthearted. And enough fat grams to give any cardiologist palpitations. Which is why the Five-Alarm is only a once-in-a-while indulgence."

He lifted his beer mug and held it aloft. "Well, in that case, here's to once-in-a-while indulgences."

A hint of color stained her cheeks, charming—and intriguing—him. It had been a long time since he'd seen a woman blush.

"To indulgences," she agreed, clinking her mug against his.

He sucked down a long, icy swallow, then set his glass on the colorful cardboard coaster, resisting the urge to press the cold mug to his forehead. He needed something hot as much as he needed a hole in his head, but he couldn't deny he liked a woman who wasn't afraid to eat something other than a salad. And there was no point denying that he liked this particular woman. Or that she turned him on just by sitting here— hell, she'd turned him on the first time he'd seen her. Or that her kiss had the impact of a horse kick to the head.

Definitely time to get a conversation started—before she thought he was some sort of gawking, tongue-tied, weirdo. Unfortunately he wasn't a great conversationalist on his best day. All those awkward pauses, and wondering what to say next. How was he supposed to carry on a conversation with a gal who all but made him forget his name?

Offering her a half smile, he asked, "How long have you worked here at the resort, Lexie?"

And it was as simple as that. No awkward pauses, no not knowing what to say. The next two hours whizzed by in a blur of laughter, conversation, fiery-spiced food, and a pitcher of ice water to accompany their beer. He couldn't recall the last time he'd enjoyed himself just talking to a woman. When he'd felt so at ease. It had been a long time. Too long.

Yet, for all the being at ease his mind was enjoying,

his body was having one hell of a hard time. Literally. Sexual awareness simmered between them until he felt as if he'd been stuffed into a pressure cooker. He saw it in her eyes, felt it tingle through him when their fingers touched passing the ketchup bottle. When her foot brushed his shin as she crossed her legs under the table. He wrapped his fingers around his beer mug to keep from giving in to the overwhelming desire to drag her into his lap and run his hands all over her. But every look, every smile she gave him, pushed him a little closer to the edge.

Over chili fries and wings, he learned that Lexie lived in a small house about five miles from the resort, that she loved animals, and had a cat named Scout who was fond of salmon, popcorn—buttered only—and Doritos—nacho-cheese flavor, please. She also loved baseball and classic movies, hated horror flicks and any story with a sad ending.

"I always rewrite the sad ending in my head so it's not sad anymore," she said, nibbling on a chili fry.

Watching those gorgeous lips wrap around that fry raised his temperature a good ten degrees. Feeling as if he'd burst if didn't touch her, he reached out and gently tugged on one of her chin-length, riotous curls. The soft, silky strands slid between his fingers.

"Happy endings, huh?" he murmured. "So at the end of *Gone With the Wind*...?"

It took her several seconds to answer, a fact that pleased him. Clearly she found his touch distracting. Good. Because for the past two hours she'd distracted the hell out of him.

Finally she said, "Um, Scarlett gets her man."

He continued to play with her hair. "And *West Side Story*?"

"Ah, Maria gets Tony—who, of course, doesn't die."

"What about *Hamlet?*"

"In my version, Ophelia—who, of course doesn't die—gets Hamlet—who—"

"Of course doesn't die. I'm beginning to see a pattern." He tucked several curls behind her ear, then slowly traced her jawline with a single fingertip.

She swallowed. Hard. "So, um, do all cowboys read stuff like *Hamlet?*"

"They do if it's a college course requirement."

"I remember you wore a University of Montana T-shirt the other night. Is that where you went?"

"It is." Clearly she still wanted to chat. That was fine—he liked talking to her. But no law said he had to continue making it easy for her. His finger resumed its leisurely path across her chin. "Managed to graduate, even in spite of *Hamlet.*"

"What is your degree in?"

"Chemical engineering."

She blinked twice. "You, uh, get to make much use of that expertise on the ranch?"

He laughed. "Hardly ever. Although after graduation I worked for a year at a research lab on a project geared toward developing alternate energy sources."

Her brows hiked upward, and he skimmed his fingertip over the arches, then down her smooth cheek. "Mmm, why did you work in the field for only a year?"

"Turned out I'm not much of a nine-to-five guy. I enjoyed the challenge of research, but after a while I found being cooped up in the lab too confining."

"Office work isn't my cup of tea, either. I love being outdoors too much." She shifted slightly in her seat and her eyes drifted half-closed. "That feels...nice."

"Good." He moved his explorations lower, over her

throat, to dip into the vulnerable hollow of her collarbone. Enjoying her quick intake of breath, he said, "Actually, the main reason I went to college was because my mom always wanted me to. She'd drummed the importance of education into me as early as I could remember. By the time I was in high school, I realized I wanted to go to college, wanted to try something other than bein' a cowboy. I did love the challenge and broadening my horizons, and it's nice to have a degree to fall back on, but being a cowboy is in my blood."

"That's very distracting, you know."

"What—me bein' a cowboy?"

"The way that you're touching me."

He studied her for several seconds, absorbing the delicate shiver vibrating beneath his cruising fingertips. He liked the way her skin looked next to his. Liked the soft feel of her skin under the glide of his thumb.

"Do you want me to stop?"

She shook her head. "No. I want you to tell me why a chemical engineer cowboy wants to buy a sailboat."

Taking her hands, he turned them palms upward, and while lightly caressing the pale blue crisscross of veins on her wrists, he told her. All about his dad, and the dream they'd shared to someday sail around the Mediterranean together, and how that dream was cut short by his father's death.

"So I'm going to do it myself," he concluded. "For me, and for my dad. It won't be the same without him, but I know he'll be up in heaven cheering me on."

She entwined her fingers with his and gently squeezed. "You really loved him."

"I did. He was a great man. If I manage to be half the man he was, I'll consider that I've done real well."

An expression he couldn't decipher flickered in her

eyes. "You realize that attempting such a voyage is dangerous, even for an experienced sailor."

"And that's why I'm here. To gain the experience I need."

"You'll require more knowledge than you can cram into a few weeks, Josh."

"Maybe. But I have to start somewhere. And you're just the gal to teach me everything I need to know."

Her gaze flicked down to where his thumbs drew slow circles on her palms. "I suspect that you already know plenty."

He pulled their entwined hands to his mouth and pressed a kiss to the inside of her wrist. "I know what I want."

Heat, mixed with a wicked gleam, kindled in her eyes. "Do you want to know what *I* want?"

"Like you wouldn't believe."

She leaned forward, pulling their joined hands toward her mouth. "I want to play a game. Do you like games?" she whispered against his fingers.

"I do. What kind of game did you have in mind?"

"It's called 'now it's my turn.' Would you like to know how I ended up working here at the Whispering Palms?"

"Darlin', I want to hear anything you want to tell me."

Pure deviltry stared back at him, and she began caressing his fingers, one by one, gently stroking their length. Her action was so blatantly sexual, she might as well have been stroking his penis. 'Cause for damn sure his body's reaction was the same.

"I landed here by way of almost a dozen air force bases all around the country," she said, and it took all his concentration to focus on her words. "My father was a career man, so every couple of years, *phffft!*—" she snapped her fingers "—we moved. The older I got, the more I hated being uprooted. Of all the places Dad was stationed, Florida was my favorite. I love the outdoors, the weather, the beach—all of it."

She paused, and with her eyes steady on his, she brought his palm to her lips. He held his breath, anticipating the feel of her lips against his skin. Instead she touched her tongue to his palm, forcing a moan from him.

"Do you want me to stop?"

"Hell, no."

He could actually feel his eyes glaze over as she continued her story, all the while alternately kissing, nibbling and flicking her tongue over his fingers.

"I attended the University of Miami and earned my teaching degree. But after three years teaching elementary school, I accepted the job here." With her gaze locked on his, she sucked the tip of his index finger into the heat of her mouth, damn near stopping his heart. He endured her tongue circling his fingertip until he thought he'd explode, then he slipped his finger from her mouth and skimmed it over her bottom lip.

"Working at the resort is perfect," she said, her soft lips brushing against his finger with each word, "because I can combine teaching, which I love, with the outdoors and sports."

"Is your dad still in the air force?"

"No. He retired three years ago. He and Mom 'live'—" she made air quotes with her fingers "—in Maryland, but they're rarely home. They bought an RV and spend most of their time traveling around the country. This week they're in Arizona."

"Sounds like fun."

"They enjoy their nomadic lifestyle. Me, I've done enough wandering around to last me a lifetime."

She settled his hands palms up on the table, splayed his fingers, then proceeded to slowly trace her fingertips over calloused skin that he'd never known was so sensitive.

Silence fell between them, which was just as well because her "now it's my turn" game had shot his ability to make chitchat all to hell. Unable to endure the sweet torture she was inflicting on his palms any longer, he captured her hand and raised it to his mouth, pressing a heated kiss to the flower-scented inside of her wrist. Her lips parted and he absorbed the quickening of her pulse against his lips.

She was lovely. And smart. And had him aroused as hell. Him—Josh Maynard, regular guy. Not Josh Maynard, rodeo star. There wasn't an ounce of artifice or being celebrity-struck in her gaze. Only admiration and genuine interest—sentiments he returned—and enough heat to make him feel as if he were roasting over a barbecue pit.

Lexie looked across at Josh, his dark eyes watching her over their joined hands, her wrist tingling from the warm press of his lips, her body humming from his featherlight touches, and she had to forcibly recall how to breathe. *In with the good air, out with the bad air.*

Okay. Over the past two hours of beer and artery-clogging food, she'd found out that Josh Maynard was not only painfully attractive, but articulate, intelligent, amusing and had cared deeply for both his parents. She liked him. He wasn't a wacko, thank goodness, and had the sexiest smile she'd ever seen. The mere brush of his fingers against her skin had her libido dancing the cha-

cha, and his hands were really, *really* sexy. Strong yet sensitive.

She wanted those hands on her.

And if there was any man on the planet who could kiss better than him, God bless the woman who found him. Josh not only had a beautiful mouth, he knew how to use it.

She wanted that mouth on her.

Everything masculine about him had everything feminine in her waving white flags of surrender. No doubt about it, he was the perfect fun, wild, temporary guy to end her long bout with celibacy and to catapult her back into the social swing. He was definitely Mr. Fling.

Lisa paused at their table and left the check. "You two need anything else?"

Privacy. "No, thanks, Lisa," Lexie said. Before she could reach for the check, Josh pulled it toward him and scribbled his name across the bottom, charging the amount to his room.

"I invited *you*," Lexie protested. "This was supposed to be my treat."

"Aw, a cowboy can't let a lady buy his beer. Think of the ribbing I'd get around the campfire."

"Like you already get for your snakebite?"

"Exactly." He cocked a single brow. "Wanna see my scar?"

His tone was light but there was no mistaking the husky note of arousal in his voice or the underlying meaning behind his question. Leaning forward, she looked him right in the eye and whispered, "Yeah. I do."

His eyes darkened, filling with heat and promise. "My place or yours?"

"Yours is closer."

He slid across the booth, stood, then held out his hand. Without breaking eye contact, she slid her hand into his.

JOSH CONGRATULATED himself on his self-control while walking her across the lobby—not an easy walk with his jeans nearly strangling him. And a nearly impossible amount of time to wait to touch her. Kiss her. What was it about this woman that had him so undone? So captivated? Had him wanting her as he'd never wanted another woman? And damn it, he should know, 'cause he'd sure as hell wanted his fair share.

Another couple stepped into the elevator with them, giving him a moment to collect himself, to get his desire under control. Indeed, by the time he shut the door to his room behind them, he had everything back in perspective. Sure he liked her, sure she was desirable, but that was it. A healthy case of lust. On both sides. They'd enjoy each other tonight, hell maybe for the duration of his stay here, and then they'd go their separate ways. No mess, no fuss, no interruption or complication of his plans. Perfect. His inner voice snickered, *Yeah, right,* but he managed to ignore it.

He slid the door bolt into place, then crossed the room to stand in front of Lexie, who stood at the foot of the king-size bed, looking at the floor. Uh-oh. Clearly she'd also spent those few minutes in the elevator thinking. Touching one finger under her chin, he gently raised her face until their eyes met.

"Second thoughts?" he asked.

"No. Yes." A short laugh pushed past her lips. "No. It's just that I'm feeling a bit discombobulated. It's, um, been a while."

Curious he asked, "How long is 'a while'?"

A flush of clear embarrassment washed over her cheeks. "Almost a year."

A soft whistle blew past his lips. "Must have been a hell of a breakup."

"Not in an acrimonious way. Actually it was more sad than anything. He was a good guy, but just not the right guy for me."

"Were you married?"

"Engaged."

"Well, he might have been a good guy, but he couldn't have been the smartest horse in the stable to let a gal like you get away. You can't let one bad apple spoil the whole bunch of bananas."

She laughed. "Now that's a mixed metaphor if I ever heard one."

"Well, that's the kind of woman you are."

"Hey, I'm a lot of things, but I am *not* a metaphor mixer."

"I meant you're the kind of woman who makes a man forget what he's saying. Forget what he's doing. Makes him all confused and—what was that word you used?"

"Discombobulated?"

"Yeah. That's what you do, all right. Get a man's ulated all discombobed." He brushed his fingertips over her smooth cheek. "Lexie, there's nothing to worry about. Making love is like riding a horse—you don't forget how."

A smile lifted up one corner of her mouth. "Bad analogy for two reasons. First, I think that 'you don't forget how' thing is about riding a *bike*."

"Not where I come from. What's the second reason?"

"I've never ridden a horse."

He couldn't hide his surprise. "You're kidding. An outdoorsy gal like you?"

"Not kidding. The opportunity just never presented itself."

"We'll have to see what we can do about that. You don't know what you're missing." He looked down into her hazel eyes. "Any other problems?"

"Condoms?"

"Got 'em."

"Well, then, I guess I'm all talked out."

"That's the best news I've heard all night." Settling his hands on her hips, he pulled her closer, until their bodies touched from chest to knee. A wave of heat washed through him, gaining momentum at the desire simmering in her gaze. Lowering his head, he brushed his lips lightly over hers. A tiny sigh escaped her, warm and spicy against his mouth. She parted her lips, and his tongue glided into the velvet heat of her mouth.

In a heartbeat their kiss turned wild, a lush, open-mouthed mating of lips and tongues. It was as if she'd hooked him up to a bunch of electrodes, then flipped the switch. Raw want scraped at him, narrowing his every thought and focus on her. Her soft, fragrant skin, the feel of her hands moving up his chest, over his shoulders, then tangling in his hair.

He ran one hand up her back, sifting his fingers into the curls brushing her nape, while his other hand wandered down to the curve of her bottom. She rose up on her toes, pressing herself more fully against him, and his erection jerked in response. Logic told him to slow down, to take his time and savor her, but unfortunately logic wasn't in charge. Besides, she was having none of it, and he wasn't about to argue. Her hands raced restlessly over him, down to his waistband, where she tugged impatiently at his T-shirt. He broke their kiss only long enough to pull it over his head. In the instant it took him to remove his shirt, she'd yanked her tank top over her head, then sent it sailing across the room.

He cupped her full breasts in his hands, gliding his thumbs over her aroused nipples. A low groan sounded in her throat, and he pulled his gaze up to her face. Her eyes were smoky with want, her lips wet and reddened from their ardent kiss. Before he could register more, she ran her palms down his chest, tickling her fingers over his abdomen, forcing a quick suck of air into his lungs. He moved forward, walking her backward, until the backs of her legs hit the foot of the bed.

Dipping his head, he ran kisses down her throat, then circled his tongue around her nipple before taking the tight bud into his mouth.

Lexie threw her head back, and simply let the sensations wash through her. An ache of deep want pulled at her, from where his mouth caressed her breast, down to her core. She felt hot, and impatient, and wanted them both naked. But his mouth was so warm and seductive, distracting her from her goal of ridding him of his jeans.

And before she could regroup, he gently urged her back until she sat on the bed. He dropped to his knees in front of her, lifting her foot to slowly remove her sandal. He caressed her bare foot, running the pad of his thumb up her instep, shooting delight up her leg. He looked up at her, and her breath caught at the concentrated heat emanating from his eyes.

"You're beautiful, Lexie," he said in a husky, aroused voice as he slipped off her other sandal.

The way he was looking at her, with those sexy eyes all hot and focused, made her feel positively woozy. Before she could return the compliment, which she surely would have if she'd been able to find her voice, he ran his hands up her legs, pushing up her full skirt until it bunched around her waist. Leaning forward, he pressed his open mouth against the sensitive skin of her inner thigh. The sight of his dark head between her legs, the brush of his tongue dampening her flesh, brought a deep groan to her throat.

"You smell so good," he whispered, his warm breath caressing her. "Like flowers. And sunshine."

He moved closer, the breadth of his shoulders spreading her legs wider. Reaching under her skirt, he eased her lace panties down her legs. Heart pounding with anticipation, she reclined back on her elbows, watching as he kissed his way slowly up her thighs, sliding his hands under her to pull her closer.

At the first touch of his mouth to her feminine flesh, her breath left her body in a rush of hot desire. Then she simply forgot how to breathe, as he lifted her against him and made love to her with his mouth, his lips and tongue caressing and gliding, delving, circling, until she was mindless. His hands, his mouth, were relentless. Unstoppable. Everywhere. She collapsed back onto the mattress, fisting her hands on the bedspread in search of an anchor as an intense orgasm throbbed through her.

While delightful aftershocks still pulsed, she felt him rise. Heard the sound of a drawer opening, then the *shush* of him removing his jeans. She pried open her eyes in time to see him rolling on a condom. Then he loomed over her, and their lips met in a voluptuous kiss. His heat, mingled with her musk, inundated her senses. With her skirt still rucked up about her waist, she spread her legs wide, lifting her hips to welcome him.

He slid into her in one long stroke, filling her. She expected fast and furious, flash and heat, but instead he stilled. Breaking off their kiss, he propped his weight on his forearms and looked down at her.

Compelling eyes, dark and intense, searched hers. She looked up at him, absorbing the sensation of him inside her. The brief thought that this interlude was supposed to be light and fun flickered through her mind. Surely it wasn't supposed to feel this...intense. Surely she wasn't supposed to feel this connection to him.

"Lexie." That single, husky-voiced word sounded faintly like a question. As if he, too, felt and wondered at this...whatever it was passing between them.

She wanted to reply, to say his name, but then he started to move, slowly rocking his hips, and she lost the ability to speak. Her eyes slid closed, and she gave herself over totally to her passion. Her hands glided down his smooth back, to his buttocks, urging him deeper, higher. Her tension escalated, then in a rush, her orgasm washed over her like a great wave. A long, deep moan vibrated in her throat and she clutched him tighter, wrapping her legs around his hips. She felt him thrust again, then he buried his face against her neck, his groan of release sounding in her ear.

Still intimately joined, she laid beneath him, sated, languid, listening to his choppy breathing as she waited for her own breathing to regulate. His weight pressed her into the mattress, and she savored the press of his chest against hers, the tickle of his chest hair against her breasts.

She felt him lift his head, and opened her eyes to

find him looking down at her with an unreadable expression.

There were about a dozen things she wanted to say, first and foremost, *Thanks, I needed that*, but lengthy speech was still beyond her. So she said the one word she could manage.

"Wow."

He studied her in silence for several seconds, then nodded. "Yeah." He touched the tip of his tongue to his lower lip. "You taste like flowers. Everywhere."

Heat swept through her. "Well, you would know."

"That's some spark that's between us."

"Definitely shorted out all my circuits." She raised her hands above her head and stretched like a contented cat. Then she ran her index finger over his lovely bottom lip. "You know, in the body-score-keeping scheme of things, you know a lot more about me than I know about you. And now that I can breathe again, I think it's about time I evened up the score."

"Consider me at your disposal."

"So, uh, what's your recovery time looking like?"

"Definitely gonna need a few minutes."

"Would a massage help?"

"Depends on what you plan to massage. What are you thinking?"

"I'm thinking about you, me and a nice warm shower. What are you thinking?"

A slow grin eased across his face. "That great minds think alike."

"HEY, there's no scar on your ass."

Josh pushed his wet hair from his eyes, then looked over his shoulder. Lexie stood behind him, shower spray bouncing off her shoulders, bar of soap in hand.

Her eyes were narrowed on his butt, and she looked disgruntled.

"I beg your pardon?"

"Your ass." She ran a soapy hand over his buttocks and he sucked in a breath. "No scar." She looked at him with a clearly suspicious expression. "I thought you were bitten by a snake."

"I was. Right there." He touched his finger to a spot on his left buttock. "Didn't leave a scar. Snakebites usually don't." He turned around and took the soap from her.

Her gaze skimmed over his torso, lingering on his groin, which tightened in response. Then she reached out and brushed her fingertips over his upper thigh. "How did this happen?"

"All your fault, sweetheart. 'Fraid I took one look at you, and I've been hard ever since."

"The *scar*. On your leg."

"Oh. Got caught by a Brahman horn."

Her eyes widened. "Brahman? As in bull?"

"Don't know of any other kind."

She ran her fingers down the length of the thin seven-inch scar. "Aren't those bulls wild and vicious? What were you doing so close to one?"

"I was ridin' him in a rodeo. Or rather, I was trying to ride him. Without much success, unfortunately, as that scar can attest."

She stared at him with an expression he couldn't recall any other woman ever looking at him with, especially when he mentioned riding in the rodeo. Instead of interest and admiration, Lexie looked downright horrified. "Rodeo? You ride in *rodeos*?"

Hmm. Her reaction piqued his curiosity, but at the moment, other things were much more interesting.

Such as that trio of golden freckles dusting the base of her throat. Brushing a single fingertip over the marks he said, "You say 'rodeo' like I kicked small dogs and stole social security checks from elderly ladies. Most cowboys try their hand at the rodeo at least once."

"Isn't it very dangerous?"

"It is. But I don't do it anymore." That was certainly true. He was officially retired. "Now, I can think of at least ten other things I'd rather be doing than talking. Like playing a game of Shampoo, for instance."

"Sounds interesting. How do you play?"

"I get you all in a lather. Then rinse and repeat." To demonstrate, he leaned forward and kissed her.

When he lifted his head, she murmured, "Hmm. Nice kiss. I give it a 9.4."

"Nine point four? Hell." He stepped forward, backing her against the wall. Shower spray rained down on them as he pressed against her, his erection sliding against her soapy belly. "Hang on, sweetheart. We're going for a ten."

5

LEXIE SPENT THE ENTIRE next day trying to do two things: not watch the clock and not think about Josh.

She failed miserably on both accounts.

Not only did her eyeballs constantly stray to her watch, but each time her mind performed a quick calculation, then registered its report. *Only twelve hours and fourteen minutes till you see him again... Only eleven hours and forty-two minutes... Only nine hours and eight minutes....*

If she had a nickel for every time she scanned the pool and beach areas for him, she'd be in Bill Gates's league. And it was totally ridiculous to even scan for him since he'd told her he planned to spend the day checking out sailboats. It was fortunate she knew the routine at the resort by rote, because her mind was simply not on her job. No, her mind was too busy reliving last night...and anticipating tonight.

An image of her and Josh in the shower flashed in her mind and she had to take a deep breath. He might have been going for a "ten," but he had delivered a twelve. At least. More like a fifteen. Had any man ever looked so good all wet and soapy? Felt so good? Made her feel so good?

Nope. On all counts. No doubt about it, Josh was an amazing and generous lover. She couldn't have picked a better guy to have a fling with.

But somewhere between them making mind-blowing use of the second and third condoms, her pesky inner voice had started dropping unsettling, unwanted raindrops on her parade—raindrops that soon plopped on her head like water balloons. Yes, she'd felt sated and languid and feminine and incredibly satisfied. But there was something else sneaking in—a not-so-welcome feeling she recognized with a sense of dawning unease.

Tenderness.

Damn it, she didn't want warm, cozy, tender feelings raising their unwanted heads! And she certainly didn't want this transient vacationing cowboy to inspire them. There was absolutely no room for warm fuzzies in this equation. Good grief, what was wrong with her? A couple of orgasms and she was totally losing her grip.

Knowing that the best thing she could do was to put some space between them, she'd left shortly after the fourth condom. Obviously she was incapable of thinking clearly when he was close. Especially when he was lying on top of her, naked and still buried deep in her body. He'd asked her to stay, and the fact that it would have been so easy to do so, convinced her it was imperative that she leave. But they had a swimming lesson scheduled for tonight. And as much as her mind cautioned her to remain aloof, she couldn't wait.

Without a doubt, last night had been… Holy cow. She didn't know. Incredible. Exciting. But something else. Something more and unsettling that she couldn't put her finger on. Had he felt it, too?

Don't be ridiculous. It was sex. Great sex. That's all. You're reading too much into it because it had been so long, you'd forgotten what it felt like. How good it could be.

Yet even as that thought occurred to her, her little inner voice piped up, *It's never been that good. That hot.*

With an effort she forced her attention back to the task at hand and stored away the flippers and masks from her snorkeling excursion, then made her way toward the Marine Patio for a quick lunch.

After placing her order for a turkey club, another image of her and Josh together in the shower, her pressed up against the tiles, legs wrapped around his waist as he thrust deep inside her, flashed in her mind. She squeezed her eyes shut in a futile effort to dispel the image. If she didn't get ahold of herself and her runaway libido, she'd be tempted to track him down, looking for a nooner.

Hey, now that's not a bad idea, her unruly hormones chimed in.

She pressed her lips together in annoyance and told her hormones to sit down and shut up. Clearly she was suffering from a glandular imbalance brought on by too much sudden sex after such a long drought.

She managed to nab a table under an umbrella—lord knew she was hot enough without the glaring sun beating down on her—and had just taken a bite of her sandwich when a familiar feminine voice sounded behind her.

"There you are!" Darla slid into the bright aqua-and-yellow chair opposite her. She pulled off her designer shades, then gave Lexie's face a thorough, narrow-eyed exam. Lexie, wishing she'd kept her own shades firmly on her nose, tried her best to keep her features impassive, but clearly she failed for a knowing smile eased across Darla's face.

"I knew it," Darla said, filching a pickle from Lexie's plate. "And if it weren't for the fact that I'm happy for

you and that your brain is clearly bamboozled by outrageously fabulous sex, I'd be royally pissed that you
didn't call me. For crying out loud, I've been dying all
morning, waiting to hear from you." She bit the pickle
spear in two and raised her brows. "So...don't keep me
in suspense. Clearly you decided he wasn't a wacko or
a creep. And based on that neon glow radiating off you,
he's stupendous in bed."

Heat rushed into her cheeks. "Yes. To all of the
above."

"How stupendous?"

A sigh she couldn't contain eased past her lips. "Off
the charts. He gave me goose bumps in places you can't
even see with a mirror. And that's before he even took
off his clothes."

Darla's eyes goggled, and the other pickle half
dropped from her fingers onto the table. "Tell me he
has a brother. Please."

"Sorry. Only child."

"Damn." She heaved a mournful sigh, but then
brightened. "Well, the rest of womanhood's loss is your
gain. When are you seeing him again?"

"Tonight. We have a swimming lesson."

"And after the lesson?"

A picture of Josh, naked and aroused, rose in her
mind's eye. "We didn't specifically discuss it, but I
wouldn't turn down the chance of a repeat of last
night."

"Was Mr. Cowboy as blown away by your night together as you were?"

"I didn't hear any complaints. In fact, his enthusiasm
was extremely flattering."

Something in her tone must have sounded less nonchalant than she'd hoped for because Darla's eyes narrowed. "But something's bothering you."

"Not really. It's just that..." She shrugged. "Naturally I was hoping he'd be nice. I just hadn't expected him to be so *extremely* nice."

"Nice as in 'nice body, nice ass, nice technique' or nice as in 'nice guy, nice smile, nice personality'?"

"Well, both. But option number two is the one that surprised me."

Darla nodded sagely. "Ah. So you like him. And that worries you." Before Lexie could answer, Darla reached out and squeezed her hand. "Listen, Lex. It's perfectly natural that you'd like him. You *should* like him. You wouldn't have gone to bed with him if he wasn't a decent man. So don't sweat it and get all crazed over it. He's handsome and sexy and great in bed and nice. What's not to like? You're having a fling, nothing more. Remember the rules. Fun, wild and *temporary*. He's Mr. Transition, getting you back into the groove, building up your confidence, so that when Mr. Right comes along, your engine's all revved up and ready. Just keep things in perspective and enjoy yourself."

Some of the tension eased from Lexie's shoulders. Darla was right. She just needed to keep things in perspective. She was simply out of practice when it came to stuff like this—although, she'd never been in practice with brief affairs. There'd only been two other men besides Tony—one in college and one during her first year teaching—and both of those relationships had lasted over a year.

Yup, she just needed to get into the swing of things, and, as Darla said, enjoy herself. And as long as she kept any emotions from sneaking into the mix, all would be well. After all, how difficult could that be?

JOSH STOOD IN THE POOL, arms outstretched and resting along the bumpy cement edge, cool water lapping at his waist. He refused to check his watch again, logic telling him that no more than thirty seconds had elapsed since the last time he'd looked at it, and a good ten minutes remained before their lesson was scheduled to start. And he also refused to look down at the front of his swimsuit, which, no matter how he tried to will it otherwise, remained tented.

Damn, why wasn't the cool pool water taking the edge off his ardor? A humorless laugh whooshed past his lips. Hell, cool water didn't stand a chance. What he needed was ice water. And somehow, he suspected even that wouldn't help. No doubt about it, he was hot and bothered, and it was all her fault.

He tipped his head back and squeezed his eyes shut. The same question that had plagued him all day echoed once again in his brain. What the hell had happened last night?

Sex, you idiot. Great sex in fact. Best you've had in a while.

A frown pulled on his brow. A while? How about *ever*.

And just sex? Nope.

He had enough experience to know that a hell of lot more than sex had happened between him and Lexie. And, as tempted as he might be to do so, there was no point in lying to himself about it. Years ago Dad had given him some advice he'd taken to heart. *Son, the biggest liar you'll ever have to face is the one who watches you shave in the mirror every morning.*

Well, he might be able to squeak a falsehood past

himself now and again, but this was not one of those times. The truth was like a horseshoe smacking him upside his head. What the hell had happened last night?

He'd fallen in love.

Yup, after a day spent pondering, there was no doubt. He'd fallen ass over spurs in love. He hadn't been looking, but love had bitten him right on the ass. Damn. Story of his life, gettin' bit on the ass when he wasn't lookin'. He'd been around the block too many times not to know that what he felt for Lexie was special. And different—stronger than anything he'd felt for any other woman. This was a *need*. A *want* that went beyond sex. She inspired an unfamiliar protectiveness and an overwhelming urge to know everything about her. What she'd been like growing up. Her favorite color. Favorite food. What made her laugh. During their conversation last night, he'd liked all the things he'd learned about her, and they'd just whetted his appetite for more.

Another one of Dad's sage tidbits tapped him on the shoulder. *It don't take a genius to spot a Thoroughbred filly in a flock of sheep, 'cause you don't see one there all too often. Just takes a lucky man.*

Lexie's smiling face rose in his mind and he shook his head. The last thing he'd been looking for when he came here was a standout in the crowd, but he'd stumbled upon one just the same. Yup, he'd been in over his head the minute he'd clapped eyes on her, and last night had just sealed the deal for him. Just like his dad, he'd fallen in love at first sight.

But damn, the timing was rotten. He'd come here for one reason—to learn what he needed so he could fulfill the dream he and Dad hadn't been able to fulfill together. So he could put that part of his life behind him and find some peace of mind. Romance, let alone falling in love, had most definitely not figured into his plans or his timetable.

You know what they say about the best laid plans...

And not only did the timing stink, but the location was certainly less than stellar. Hell, he was a couple thousand miles from home. From his ranch and the people who depended on him for their livelihoods. And he was only here for the next few weeks. No, findin' a gal like Lexie here and now was a complication he hadn't banked on. And as if there weren't enough roadblocks already, there was Lexie herself to consider. He clearly sensed she wasn't looking for any sort of serious entanglement, and even if she were, she wouldn't choose a guy who only planned to be around for a few weeks. No, he'd bet his bottom dollar that to her, last night had been nothing more than a fling—a way to end her nearly year-long sabbatical from sex.

A humorless laugh escaped him. Unbelievable. For the first time in his life he'd fallen in love, and the object of his affections only wanted him for sex. How ironic was *that?*

Well, he could play it cool. No need to tip his hand yet. He was a patient man, willing to give her some time to fall in love with him. As long as she didn't take too damn long about it.

A soft splash caught his attention and he opened his eyes. Lexie was walking slowly down the curved steps into the water. Their eyes met, and damn if it didn't feel as if he'd taken a sucker punch to the gut. Annoyed with himself for wanting to just reach out and grab her like some primitive caveman or uncouth, horny teenager, he kept his arms spread and gripped the edge of the pool for all he was worth.

She waded toward him with a half-shy, half-knowing expression that aroused a lot more than just his interest. Her dark brown hair surrounded her head in curly abandon, and he instantly recalled the feel of its silky softness sifting through his fingers. His gaze settled on her mouth and he bit back a groan. Hands down, she possessed the most gorgeous lips he'd ever seen. And God help him, he couldn't wait to taste them again.

She stopped directly in front of him and offered him a half smile. "Hi. Hope I haven't kept you waiting long."

The newly minted certainty that he'd been waiting for her a lot longer than the ten minutes he'd been standing in the pool crept through his mind. "Just arrived myself." By God, it was nearly impossible not to snatch her into his arms. But she had said she wanted things to remain businesslike in the pool. And there was no doubt that he'd be hard-pressed to let her go once he got hold of her.

"Did you have a good day?" she asked.

His grip on the edge tightened. "Yup."

"Did you find a sailboat you liked?"

"Nope."

She cocked a brow. "Something wrong?"

Nothing that a few hours alone with you wouldn't cure. "Nope. I'm just remembering what you said last night about keeping it just to swimming lessons in the pool. Wouldn't want you gettin' all mad at me." One corner of his mouth lifted. "Figured I'd play hard to get."

"Hard to get, huh?" Reaching out, she touched one finger to the base of his throat, then slowly dragged her fingertip down the center of his chest. "How hard?"

With a groan, he yanked her into his arms. "I give up."

His mouth covered hers in a demanding, impatient kiss, filled with all the overwhelming feelings and pent-up frustration he'd felt all day. His tongue explored all the sweet secrets of her mouth, while his hands smoothed down her back to her bottom, pulling her flush against him. She moaned, wrapped her arms around his neck, pressing herself closer, and he was lost. Lost in the feel of her curves under his hands. Her soft breasts crushed to his chest.

Her flowery scent rose from her skin like tropical steam, invading his senses. Spreading his legs farther apart, he shifted, slowly rubbing his erection against the curve of her belly. A shudder ran through her, echoing in him, and it took every drop of his nearly depleted control to keep himself from simply yanking aside the thin barriers of their swimsuits and easing this relentless ache pounding through him. Unfortunately this was neither the time nor the place.

With an effort that cost him, he gentled their kiss, nibbling lightly on her lips, then raising his head. Her warm breath panted against him, and she looked as dazed and bemused as he felt.

"Holy cow," she said in a rough, raspy whisper. She took in two deep breaths, then blinked at him. "Okay, you've got to be the only cowboy who kisses like that."

"Like what?"

"In that liquefy-the-brain-cells, deplete-the-oxygen, knee-removing way."

A chuckle rumbled in his throat. "Why do you say that?"

"Because if every cowboy kissed like you, nothing *except* kissing would get done on the ranch. The entire beef and cattle industries would go right down the tubes, sending the economy into a tailspin."

He wanted to make a witty rejoinder, something to make her smile, to keep the conversation light, but when he spoke, the simple, undeniable truth tumbled out.

"I thought about you all day."

Lexie looked into his dark, serious eyes, and her heart performed a cartwheel. She certainly could say the same to him, although she briefly considered not doing so. But to lie about something so obvious, no doubt God would smite her with a lightning bolt. "I thought about you, too."

He tucked a wayward curl behind her ear, the intimate gesture tingling pleasure down her spine. "During my sailboat-shopping travels today, I ran across a country-western place not too far from here. They serve food and drinks, and there's a dance floor and a couple of pool tables, too. Would you like to go tonight, after our lesson?"

"You must mean Buffalo Pete's."

"Yeah, that was the name of it. Have you ever been?"

"Many times. It's a local favorite. The wings are hot and the beer's icy cold. I'd love to go." She smiled, then forced herself to step away from him, not easy considering everything in her wanted to remain plastered against him. "Ready for our lesson?"

"I'm ready for anything you're willin' to dish out, Miss Lexie."

She cocked a brow at him. "Are we still talking about swimming?"

His dimple flashed. "For now."

JOSH EMPLOYED the attention-focusing ability that had stood him in good stead during years of rodeo competition to concentrate on their swimming lesson. Following Lexie's directions, he practiced his breathing, then added the kickboard. Then she showed him the arm movements for the basic crawl stroke, which they practiced side by side. She then had him add the breathing, and finally, the kicking. She was patient, businesslike, and tireless, going over the movements with him again and again. Between her determination and his perseverance, by the end of the hour, he'd made it to the opposite end of the pool and back.

He stood in the shallow and swiped back his wet hair. She gave him a broad grin, then applauded.

"Great job, Josh. Ninety percent of swimming is mastering the right kick-stroke-breathing pattern, and you now have a good feel for the rhythm. From here, all you need is practice. You're certainly ready to start sailing lessons."

Unable to control his smug grin, he caught her around the waist, lifted her up and spun her around. She grasped his shoulders and laughed.

He lowered her slowly, enjoying the slide of her wet body down his. "When can we start those sailing lessons, oh, great and wise teacher? Tomorrow?"

"Tomorrow is my day off."

Disappointment edged through him. "So that means you're not available?"

"Actually, it means I'm available all day."

His gaze wandered down to her full lips, and his heart thumped hard. "Now that's what I call good news."

"The best news is the great progress you've made in such a short amount of time. I think you're the best student I've ever had."

"Well, I *know* you're the best teacher I've ever had. And definitely the prettiest."

She leaned back in the circle of his arms and shot him a teasing grin. "Oh, come on. I bet there were loads of pretty science and math teachers at the University of Montana."

"There might have been, but my teachers tended toward the bearded, gray-haired, masculine variety."

"Hmm. So, me being the prettiest teacher you've ever had isn't much of a compliment considering the competition."

"Well, you're also the sexiest teacher I've ever had."

"More so than the 'bearded, gray-haired, masculine variety.' Gee, thanks."

He shot her a mock fierce frown and tightened his arms around her. "You're a tough gal to give a compliment to."

"And you're hard—"

"Because of you—"

"—to resist."

Her wicked smile fired his blood. "Well, now," he said, "that's very good to hear. I suggest we consider this lesson officially over. You still up for our date at Buffalo Pete's?"

She leaned closer and rose up on her toes to lightly tug on his earlobe with her teeth. A fog of lust enveloped him and he nearly missed her heart-stopping reply.

"Oh, I'm definitely up for it," she whispered against his ear. "For starters."

BUFFALO PETE'S was in full Saturday-night swing when they arrived shortly before 11:00 p.m. Bodies pressed three-deep at the long, polished mahogany bar, and waitresses wearing denim cutoffs, cowboy boots, and white T-shirts emblazoned with the bar's logo weaved expertly between the tables and booths. Couples swirled on the dance floor to a lively Garth Brooks tune, and the smack of billiard balls from the back room rose faintly above the noise and music.

Josh took her hand, entwining their fingers, and Lexie relished the warmth of her palm nestled against his. He led her to the hostess stand where a smiling young woman greeted them. She grabbed two plastic-coated menus, then escorted them through a labyrinth of tables toward the rear where she left them at a small table tucked in a cozy, softly lit corner. Josh held out her chair for her—an act of masculine courtesy she'd thought had gone by way of the dinosaur—then folded himself into the chair across from her.

Dressed in cowboy boots, eye-riveting snug jeans, denim shirt and a cream-colored Stetson, he certainly looked at home here, and since he wouldn't be able to hear it over the noise, she didn't even try to contain the sigh of female appreciation the sight of him inspired. The top snap of his shirt was undone, inducing another sigh at the teasing glimpse of his tanned throat. It just made her want to crawl onto his lap, unsnap the rest of his shirt, and play peekaboo.

Prying her gaze away from that fascinating fantasy-inducer, she took in the tanned sinew of his forearms where he'd rolled back his sleeves. The man definitely had great arms. And the fact that they were half-covered again made her want to remove his shirt—with her teeth.

And there was no denying that the sight of him wearing that Stetson did weird things to her pulse rate. The way it shadowed the upper part of his face, obscuring

his eyes, yet giving her an unimpeded view of his beautiful mouth—a mouth he most definitely knew how to
use—lent him an unnervingly predatory air that kicked
up her temperature a good ten degrees.

Removing his hat, he set it on the empty seat next to
him, then skimmed his fingers through his thick, dark
hair. His gaze roamed over her with an appreciation
that zoomed a feminine tingle right down to her toes.
Good grief, he had a way of looking at her that made
her feel absolutely beautiful. Feminine. And desirable.

Reaching out, he captured her hand, then pressed a
warm kiss in her palm. "You did it again, and I've got
to know how."

She didn't have a clue what she'd done, but based on
his heated expression, she was damn glad she'd done it.
"How I did what?"

"Managed to get yourself so gorgeous in less than
half an hour."

Humph. It might not have taken her long to get ready
in the employee locker room, but before leaving her
house this morning, she'd agonized over what outfit to
bring—something she *never* did. After trying on a
dozen different things, she'd finally decided upon a
simple turquoise sundress and matching sandals. The
sleeveless dress was fitted on the top, dipped low in the
back, and flared into a full skirt that ended several
inches above her knees. Of course, *he* didn't need to
know she'd fretted and worried over what to wear as if
they were attending a state dinner at the White House.

She smiled across at him. "I've never been the spend-
an-hour-getting-ready type. I wear more sunscreen
than makeup, and I gave up long ago trying to tame my
hair since it does whatever it wants no matter how
much I fuss with it. With the heat and humidity here in

Florida, in order to keep my sanity, I've become pretty low maintenance. What you see is what you get."

He touched his tongue to the center of her palm. "Promise?"

The waitress suddenly appeared at the table, sparing Lexie the need to reply, which was probably just as well since his question and the touch of his tongue had rendered her mute. While Josh ordered beer, wings and nachos, Lexie nodded her assent and took several much needed deep breaths. Good grief, at this rate, with the way he affected her breathing, she'd hyperventilate before their drinks arrived.

She glanced up at their waitress, and noticed that the young woman was staring at Josh with an odd expression, one that almost seemed to border on awe. Not that Lexie could blame her—he was pretty awe-inspiring. But really, this woman was being just a tad obvious.

Josh, however, appeared oblivious, and handed her the menus with a friendly smile, then returned the full wattage of his attention back on Lexie.

"So tell me," he said, recapturing her hand, "is what I see really gonna be what I get? 'Cause I gotta tell you, Miss Lexie, you look so hot in that dress, Buffalo Pete is going to have to take the batteries out of his smoke alarms." His eyes again wandered over her. "How is it that a gal like you has remained unattached for a year? I can only figure there's something wrong with the men around here—sunstroke or hit on the head with coconuts or something."

Warmth spread through her at his compliment. "My energies have been focused on things other than my social life. But I've managed to work in a few dates, compliments of my friend Darla who keeps trying to fix me up. Disasters, all of them." She looked toward the ceiling and shook her head. "Yes, I'm quite the expert on first dates. Unfortunately, I know next to nothing about second dates."

"This is our second date, and you're doing just fine."

"I suspect you're just easy to please."

"Actually, I'm extremely choosy."

"Besides, we're not really dating."

His brows shot upward. "No? Where I come from, this is called a date."

"Well, I suppose technically this is a date, but I wouldn't say we're dating."

"What would *you* say we're doing?"

There was something in his tone, in the underlying seriousness, watchfulness, lurking behind the playfulness that set up a fluttering in her stomach. "Well, the very temporary nature of our...arrangement...places it more in the category of a...fling."

He studied her for several seconds with an unreadable expression, and she found herself holding her breath. But then he said, "I see. I suppose you're right."

For reasons she couldn't explain and refused to examine, his agreement disappointed her.

Oh, come on, Lexie. What did you expect him to say? That he'd chuck his life in Manhattan, Montana, and stay here so you could date?

His fingers lightly caressed the length of hers, recalling her attention. "So tell me about one of these disastrous first dates."

"Ugh. They were all bad. But the worst was this past winter." She leaned forward and confided, "He had this weird breast fetish."

"I hate to break this to you, sweetheart, but lots of guys do."

"Not *my* breasts. *His* breasts. He kept touching them,

feeling and pinching them. Like he was tuning in the knobs on an old-fashioned radio. He wanted me to suck on them."

"Well, him wanting you to suck them isn't *that* weird."

"We were on the dance floor at his company's holiday party."

"Oh. That's weird."

She shook her head. "Being with my ex for so long, I was out of practice in the dating pool. But every time I attempted to dip my toe back in, I found myself surrounded by sharks and other assorted bottom feeders. I finally decided it wasn't worth the hassle—at least until someone who seemed normal happened along."

A slow smile lifted one corner of his mouth. "So I guess I seemed normal, huh?"

"Well, at least you don't have 'pyscho' stamped on your forehead. And we've been here a good ten minutes without you asking me to suck on your boobs."

"Night's still young."

She shot him a stern look, then added, "And you haven't asked me to bungee jump, shoot the Amazon, or swim with the alligators. Yeah, you seem normal enough."

"Well, there's no denyin' I'm glad I happened along. But what's this about bungee jumping and alligators? More first-date disasters?"

"No. I was referring to my ex-fiancé. I'm afraid he was something of a daredevil."

"He swam with *alligators?*"

"Yup. Wrestled them, too. And dove off cliffs. Jumped out of airplanes. Mountain climbed. Surfed during hurricanes. And that was just the tip of the iceberg. He was a total adrenaline junkie. Made Evil Knievel look like a preschool act."

"And he broke things off with you because you wouldn't join him in his crazy adventures?"

"No, I broke off with him because I couldn't take it anymore. Couldn't stand spending any more nights in the emergency room. Couldn't handle my heart stopping every time the phone rang because I knew the next phone call would be the one from the police telling me he was dead. Or paralyzed. He tried, he really did, for me, to confine his adventures to less dangerous activities, but within a month he was miserable. And that made me miserable. So he went back, with a vengeance. Won some regional competitions in a variety of extreme sports—nearly killing himself in the process. When he fell in with a lifestyle that included other women, I couldn't tolerate it any longer."

"If he wasn't your type, why'd you get engaged to him?"

"When we first started dating, then fell in love, he wasn't so...intense. He was sweet and thoughtful. But as his thirtieth birthday approached, he went through some sort of early midlife crisis. He took on increasingly reckless, dangerous adventures—as if he had to prove something to himself. I loved him, but I knew he'd never change. He'd always be wanting, needing, searching for the next challenge, while I'd always be worried and filled with dread. Success changed him, and once the womanizing started, that was it. For both our sakes, I let him go."

"Do you still love him?" he asked quietly.

"No. I pray for his safety, but I've never regretted breaking our engagement." A self-conscious laugh pushed past her lips. "And that's no doubt more about me than you ever wanted to know."

"Actually, that doesn't even break the surface of what I'd like to know about you."

His intense look arrowed fire down to her toes, and she forced herself to keep the conversation light, not to read too much into his words or expression. "Well, that's all you get to know for now 'cause it's your turn. How come a guy who looks like you doesn't have a girlfriend? Or do you have one?"

He lifted a brow, and said in a cool voice, "I don't have a girlfriend. I'm not the sort of man who would have a fling if there was someone waiting at home for me."

Heat rushed into her face at her obvious faux pas. "I'm sorry. I didn't mean to insult you. It's just that men who look like you are usually attached."

"I am completely unattached."

"Never been married?"

"Never even come close."

Hmm. Clearly commitment-phobic. Typical. As if he'd read her thoughts, he said, "Not because I'm afraid of commitment. I've just never met the right woman. And in my line of work, with all the traveling, it's pretty hard to maintain a steady relationship." He chuckled. "I've had my fair share of bad first dates, too."

Confusion tugged her brows down. "Traveling? Where do cowboys travel to? Other ranches?"

Wariness entered his eyes, and he scraped his free hand through his hair. "Well, actually, I haven't been doin' much ranching the past few years. I've spent the bulk of my time—"

The waitress's arrival cut off his words and Lexie's

imagination ran wild. What had he been doing? Something involving traveling. Great. He probably worked for the CIA, going undercover to unearth crimes in America's heartland. Probably got shot at on a daily basis. Or maybe he was a pilot—and had three wives in different cities around the globe.

Or maybe he's simply a nice, decent man, who, incredible as it may seem, is single, heterosexual, and interested in you.

As the waitress set their drinks and plates of food on the table, Lexie couldn't help but again notice that she was staring at Josh as if he were a succulent morsel and she was starving. When she'd laid down the last dish, she said in a breathless rush, "You're Josh Maynard. I'd recognize you anywhere."

Lexie's brows crept up in surprise. Oh, boy. Hopefully this woman didn't recognize Josh from the FBI's Most Wanted poster at the post office.

Josh smiled at the young woman and stuck out his hand. "Yes, ma'am. I'm Josh Maynard. Nice to meet you, Miss—?"

Lexie feared the girl might go down like a tenpin as she clasped Josh's hand. "Baker. Vickie Baker. Ohmigod. I *told* Sally and the other girls it was you, but they didn't believe me. Can I have your autograph?"

"I'd be honored, Vickie. 'Fraid I don't have a pen, though."

"I have one." She yanked her apron askew in her zeal to remove it from her pocket. A frown creased her forehead. "But all I have is my order pad to write on. Would you wait while I get a decent piece of paper?"

"I'll be right here."

Vickie gushed out another, "Ohmigod," then sped away. Josh turned to Lexie with a sheepish grin. She stared at him for several seconds until she located her voice.

"Okay, so what are you, a country singing star?"

"No. Remember how I mentioned last night that I'd done some rodeo?"

"Yes. That's how you got your scar."

"Right. Well, truth of the matter is, I've spent a fair amount of time on the rodeo circuit, and managed to make a bit of a name for myself."

"What's a 'fair amount of time'?"

"I rode some in high school and college, but except for that year doing research, the rodeo is how I've made my living since college."

"And you're how old now?"

"Thirty-four."

"And I'm guessing that since Vickie recognized you and gushed over you as if Mel Gibson *and* Brad Pitt had just strolled in, you did a little more than make a 'bit' of a name for yourself."

He shrugged. "I won a few."

"A few what? Blue ribbons?"

"World championships."

Her eyes widened. "So you're some sort of rodeo celebrity?"

"I suppose. In certain circles." He flashed her a grin. "But hey, how famous can I be? You'd never heard of me."

"Maybe because I know squat about the rodeo."

"I'd be happy to tell you anything you might want to know."

"Why didn't you mention this before now?"

His gaze searched hers. "It hadn't really come up in conversation. I retired from the circuit a few months ago. And to tell you the truth, it was nice to be with someone who didn't know. Who didn't make a fuss about it."

An image of adoring female fans "making a fuss" over Josh flashed in Lexie's mind, followed by the taunting phrase "been there, done that." "Does the rodeo have groupies—like rock and roll bands?"

"Groupies, fans, corporate endorsers," he said.

Any further elaborations he might have planned to make were cut off by the arrival of Vickie and three other young waitresses.

"I told you it was him," Vickie said with a smug grin to her cohorts. She turned to Josh. "This is Sally, Trish and Amy."

Josh nodded at the women and smiled. "Nice to meet you, ladies. And this is Lexie."

All four women said, "Hey," in greeting, but their attention was focused on Josh with the sort of zeal a jewel thief would bestow upon the Hope diamond.

"I told Ben, the bartender, that you were here," Vickie said, "and he about split a gut. He's holed up in the boss's office, printin' off some pictures of you from the Internet so you can sign 'em and we can hang 'em behind the bar."

One of the other women—Lexie believed it was the one named Amy—craned her neck around. "Are you wearing one of your All-Around buckles, Josh?" she asked in a breathless voice.

"As a matter of fact, I am."

"Oo-hh! Can we see it?"

"Sure." He scooted his chair out, then stood. Lexie noted that four pairs of female eyes zeroed in like laser beams on his big belt buckle. And all four women looked as if they'd like to polish that big brass buckle—with their tongues.

With a flip of his wrist, he removed the buckle and handed it to Amy who accepted the shiny piece as if it were the Holy Grail. The four women crowded around, oohing and aahing. Josh shot Lexie a sheepish grin and mouthed "Sorry." She waved her hand, indicating it was no problem, then she simply sat back and watched, half amazed, half amused, as he proceeded to charm the women with several rodeo anecdotes while signing autographs for them. Ben the bartender joined the group, Internet print-out pictures in hand, and Lexie watched Josh scrawl his name across images of himself atop huge, bucking Brahman bulls.

Her stomach flipped at the eye-widening images in those photos, and she gave herself a mental slap on the forehead. Good grief, so much for meeting a man who wasn't another adrenaline junkie! She could sum up what was depicted on those printouts in two words: insane. The thought stilled her. Yes, it was insane. And dangerous. And based on the behavior of these waitresses, woman clearly flocked around him like geese. Good Lord, he was just like Tony.

But did it really matter? No, of course not. She wasn't going to *marry* him. She wasn't even dating him!

He was temporary. A fling. A way to regain her confidence and to ease herself back into the singles scene, and as an added bonus, to pick up some extra money for teaching him on the side. It didn't matter that he'd spent years being tossed onto the ground by two-ton beasts, or that women hung on him like mold on cheese. Her heart was not involved. Yup, everything was now settled back into its proper perspective.

It wasn't long before curious patrons started looking toward the group gathered around their table and came over to check out what was happening. Soon a crowd had formed, men and women alike, all anxious to get an autograph and to shake Josh's hand. He was unerringly polite and patient, chatting, signing, even posing for pictures with several people who had cameras with them. He frequently squeezed Lexie's hand, smiling at her in an apologetic way, but she assured him she was fine. He introduced her to the crowd as "his friend" Lexie, and she noted that several women in the crowd raked their gazes over her in a way that indicated they'd like to take her out back and fling her in the Dumpster.

She couldn't help but admire his attitude toward all these strangers. He was charming and friendly, but even though, in spite of her presence, a number of the women flirted outrageously with him—what was she, invisible?—Josh remained merely friendly and polite in return, not rising to any of the overtures, innuendos or invitations issued to him. She couldn't deny she appreciated the courteous gesture. It definitely wasn't the way Tony would have handled a similar situation.

After he'd signed an autograph for everyone who wanted one, and Vickie had shooed off the crowd, saying, "Okay, let's leave the poor man to his evening," he turned to Lexie.

"I'm sorry that took so long, but I hate to disappoint fans. They're a loyal group, and without them, I wouldn't have had a job."

"Please, don't apologize. I enjoyed watching you." She shook her head. "It's like being out with a movie star. That one man referred to you as the Michael Jordan of rodeo!"

He shrugged. "A reporter called me that once, and after the media picked it up, it sort of stuck."

Leaning forward, she looked into his eyes. "That entire thing was amazing, but what I find most amazing of all is how modest you are about your accomplishments."

"I can't deny I'm proud of them, but I guess I don't talk about them much, especially away from the circuit. If I talk about it with other cowboys, it's business. If I talk about it with anyone else, it seems like braggin'."

"Certainly no one could blame you—you have plenty to brag about."

He reached out and clasped both her hands. "Let me tell you something. The first few years I was on the circuit, I played it for all it was worth. I was young, talented, and I enjoyed all the perks that came with winning—including the adoration. But the more I won, the more my celebrity grew, and it eventually got to the point where I didn't know if someone liked me for *me*—or because of my fame.

"I stayed with the rodeo because I love it. Love the challenge and competition. But I realigned my priorities, and a few years ago I took a big step backward from the 'fame' side of it. I'm grateful for the fan support and I'll always take the time to chat or sign an autograph. But I have to admit, it didn't bother me one bit that you didn't know who I was."

"Does that mean I shouldn't ask for your autograph?" she teased.

He slipped his hand under the table, then ran it up her thigh. "I can think of a few places I'd like to sign my name on you."

And she could think of a few more. "Why did you retire?"

"It was time. I'd accomplished everything I'd set out to—even more. Besides, my body couldn't take it much longer. My dad had died, leaving me solely responsible for the ranch we'd bought together..." His voice trailed off and he shrugged. "Like I said, it was time."

"I heard one man ask you if you planned to come out of retirement to 'even the score.' What did he mean?"

"He was referring to my last competition. I came in second place to Wes Handly, one of my biggest rivals."

"Which you didn't like."

"Can't say I did. Not that Wes didn't deserve to win. He's a good man and he outrode me. It was just hard to go out that way."

"So, would you come out of retirement?"

"Nope. I've hung up my spurs for good."

A sense of relief she didn't want to feel or examine eased through her. But a small inner voice whispered, *Yeah, and Michael Jordan retired for good, too. Several times.* Oh, yeah, it was a very good thing that her heart wasn't involved in this fling. *Fun, wild and temporary.*

Her gaze fell to their plates of uneaten food. "I think our hot wings are way cold."

"Would you like me to order a fresh batch?"

She shook her head. "Why don't we have Vickie wrap these up, then we can reheat them." She raised her gaze to his. "At my place."

His eyes darkened and his fingers tightened around hers. "That's an invitation I'd be an idiot to turn down."

"And we both know you're one of those smart-guy chemical engineers."

"Ah. So you're only interested in my mind."

"Not exactly." She allowed her gaze to wander over him in a very suggestive way. "Actually, I was thinking we could play a little game."

"Mmm. You know I like games. What did you have in mind?"

"I was thinking we could play Ice Cream."

"Can't say I'm familiar with it. How do you play?"

"I lick. You melt."

He went perfectly still, smoke all but emanating from his eyes. "Let's go."

6

JOSH DROVE his rental car slowly down the winding street, one hand on the wheel, the other hand resting on the leather seat, his fingers entwined with Lexie's. Conversation consisted of Lexie giving him directions to her house, and that was fine with him as he felt pretty much incapable of making chitchat. Her sexy game invitation swirled through his mind like a tornado, whipping up a maelstrom of lust. It was all he could do to concentrate on the road. If he allowed his fantasies free rein, they'd end up in Louisiana.

In an effort to get his mind off ice cream—at least until they arrived at her house—he forced his thoughts elsewhere. As flattering as tonight's fan attention was, he certainly hadn't planned on an impromptu autograph session. At first he'd worried that Lexie would mind, but she'd taken the interruption of their evening right in stride, a fact for which he was grateful. He'd been in similar situations before where his date had gotten all huffy and pouty and jealous, and he'd spent many evenings coaxing disgruntled dates back into good humor. It was refreshing that Lexie hadn't reacted that way, even though a few of the women had made some blatantly suggestive verbal overtures. Lexie had simply smiled at him, winked at him, and even favored him with looks that clearly indicated she was proud of him, and several that made it plain sex was in his immediate future.

He risked a quick glance at her from the corner of his eye and instantly regretted it as the glimpse he caught showed her pursing her full lips.

Damn, this was bad. This woman turned him on just *sitting there.* And she was hell on his ability to concentrate. But even worse were his powerful feelings for her—a woman who'd made it very plain tonight that this was a fling and nothing more. He feared his former occupation wasn't going to help his cause any. She clearly harbored an aversion, with good reason, to guys she designated as adrenaline junkies. And while her former alligator-wrestling fiancé sounded a bit over-the-top, Josh suspected that "rodeo cowboy" probably lumped him in the same category.

Before he could ponder further she said, "My house is the second one on the right, with the porch light on."

He pulled into the driveway, then cut the engine. The house was cream-colored stucco with a small, neat yard, nestled between two similarly styled houses. After opening her car door, an act that brought a smile to her lips, she led him up the cement walkway, then into a foyer tiled in pale green.

He followed her into a pristine kitchen done in cheerful shades of green and yellow. She opened the refrigerator, then bent over to slip in the foam to-go boxes containing their food.

The way she looked, bent over, with her dress riding up the backs of her thighs, forced him to take several long careful breaths. Then she straightened, closed the fridge, and leaned back against the white door.

"Would you like to see the rest of the place?"

"Darlin', I'm anxious to see anything you might like to show me."

She smiled, then waved her arm in an arc. "Kitchen and breakfast room." She led him through an archway, then said, "Family room." The cozy room was done in shades of blue and pale yellow, with a whitewashed wood entertainment center surrounded by an over-stuffed sectional sofa. Several fitness magazines rested on a glass coffee table, alongside a large sand-filled bowl decorated with an assortment of colorful shells. Framed photos were scattered around the room, but before he could examine them, she crossed the hard-wood floor and opened the vertical blinds along the back wall. Sliding open the patio doors, she said, "Deck."

He stepped outside and was immediately engulfed in steamy tropical air. A tall wooden fence enclosed the small backyard. In one corner of the deck stood a grill. In the other—

"Hot tub," she said, pointing toward the other corner.

An image of them, together in a pool of warm, bub-bling water flashed in his mind, leaving a trail of heat in its wake.

"I love to indulge in a muscle-relaxing soak after an active day at work," she said. "The fence provides com-plete privacy from the neighboring houses."

Their eyes met, and Josh swore something passed be-tween them. Something more than the arousing possi-bilities the hot tub offered. Something warm and inti-mate and knowing.

Reaching out, she clasped his hand then led him back into the house. She brought him through the tidy kitchen, then down a short corridor, murmuring,

"Guest room, bathroom, laundry room," as they passed a trio of doors. At the end of the hallway she said, "My bedroom."

He followed her inside, then waited while she lit several candles. Like the rest of the house, her bedroom was cozy and attractive, and decorated with "beachy" touches, from the bedspread depicting various shells against a pale aqua background, to the starfish-shaped candleholders she now applied her attention to. Except for the headboard, which was brass, the furniture was pale wicker. Again he noted a number of photos resting on her dresser and night table. Wandering over to her dresser, he picked up a frame that contained a collage of four pictures.

One showed Lexie flanked by a smiling, older couple. Clearly her parents, as he could easily see the resemblance to both of them. Her dad sported a military haircut but Lexie had his firm chin. And she'd inherited her mother's eyes and glowing smile. Two of the other photos also showed Lexie with her parents, one where they were all dressed formally, the other on a golf course. The last photo was of a grinning Lexie in the water with a dolphin.

Looking up, he watched Lexie blow out the match, her lips puckered in a way that made him ache. She walked slowly toward him, her hips gently swaying, her full skirt skimming her legs. Halting beside him, she tapped on the frame. "My parents."

"Looks like you enjoy each other's company."

"Oh, we do. My folks are great. And tireless." She chuckled. "Whenever we're together, *I'm* always the one suggesting we sit down and rest for a minute."

The sharp pang of loss hit Josh. "That's how my dad was. He wasn't happy unless he was doing something." Pushing aside his sadness, he pointed to the dolphin picture. "Another relative?"

She laughed. "Swimming with the dolphins. It's an amazing experience. You might want to try it while you're in Florida."

"Thanks, but I reckon I'll pass. If you recall, the last time I went into water that wasn't in a pool, I got bit on the ass."

"Dolphins don't bite. Besides, you can't fault that snake on its taste. You've got a great ass."

He set the frame back on her dresser. "Right back at you, Miss Lexie."

Smiling, she placed her palms on his belly, then walked her fingers up his shirt. He sucked in a breath, filling his head with a combination of her floral musk and the vanilla-scented candles, which bathed the room in a soft glow.

"How do you feel?" she asked in a smoky voice. "Are you relaxed?"

"Hell, no."

"Well, Mr. All-Around Cowboy, let's see what we can do about that."

He settled his hands on her waist and pulled her against him. "Generally speakin', fancy titles and wearin' clothes in the bedroom are a waste of time."

"What is that, wisdom from some sort of cowboy handbook?"

He lowered his head and nuzzled her fragrant neck. "As a matter of fact, it is. Cowboys are well-versed in sage knowledge that's been passed down through the generations. All time-proven to be correct." A low, pleasure-filled moan vibrated in her throat, and he touched his tongue to the spot.

"In that case," she murmured, "I suggest we get you out of these clothes."

Lexie slipped her fingers into the V opening in his shirt and did what she'd been thinking about all evening. One by one, she pulled the snaps open, the gentle click the only sound besides their breathing. When she reached his belt, she pulled the shirt from his waistband, then eased the denim down his arms where it fell to the floor behind him.

Reaching out, she placed her hands on his chest, absorbing the slap of his heartbeat against her palms. She ran her hands slowly downward, enjoying the taut muscles jerking beneath her fingers and the heat simmering in his gaze as he watched her. Teasing her fingertips around the edge of his waistband, she ran her palms up his smooth back, over his shoulders and chest, then again tickled her fingers down his ridged abdomen.

He sucked in a hissing breath and the desire burning in his gaze nearly singed her. "Sweetheart, if you think that you're going to relax me doing that, you're sadly mistaken."

"Well, I suppose relaxed isn't really what I'm going for," she conceded. "Probably aroused is closer."

"Well, aroused is what you've got."

"How aroused?"

He captured her hand and pressed it to the front of his jeans. "Very aroused."

Oh, my. "How do you work this big belt buckle?"

He released her hand, then, with a flick of the wrist, removed the buckle and set it on the edge of her dresser. Her gaze wandered down to his feet. "Boots next." Moving to the edge of the bed, he sat and quickly pulled off his boots and socks.

After slipping off her sandals, Lexie walked to the bed. "Ready to play Ice Cream?"

"Like you wouldn't believe."

"Lie down."

Never taking his gaze from hers, he pushed himself back, until he was supine, his head resting on her pillow.

With her heart pounding, Lexie knelt on the mattress next to him. Reaching out, she undid the button on his jeans, then slowly lowered the zipper. He lifted his hips to assist her, and she slid the denim down and off his legs.

Clad only in his white boxer briefs, his erection straining against the soft cotton, he stole her breath. Heat sizzled through her, pooling in a hot puddle that dampened her panties. She cupped him through his underwear, running her fingers over the length of him, reveling in his long groan. He was ready, all right. But she wanted him *really* ready.

Hiking up her dress, she straddled him, settling herself against his erection. She squirmed once and spears of pleasure arrowed through her.

He reached for her, but she captured his hands, then leaned forward to gently lower them to the mattress, above his head. "Oh, no," she whispered. "Now you just relax—"

"Yeah, right."

She flicked the tip of her tongue over his earlobe. "All you have to do is melt."

He shifted, pressing his erection harder against her. "Not a problem. You haven't even started and I'm already close to a total meltdown."

"Then let me bring you the rest of the way there."

Josh closed his eyes and clamped his fingers tightly

together to keep from touching her. Then he clenched his jaw and prayed for strength.

She ran her tongue down the side of his neck, nibbling with her lips, nipping him lightly with her teeth. Everywhere she touched him, it felt as if she'd lit bonfires on his skin. She licked her way down his body with maddening leisure, her tongue circling his nipples before taking them into the moist heat of her mouth. Pleasure and need, hot and sharp, shot through him, and his fingers turned numb from clasping them so tightly.

She shifted lower, her tongue dampening a path down to his abdomen. She blew lightly on the trail and his muscles contracted. After circling his navel she shifted lower still, licking across the skin just above his waistband.

Opening his eyes, Josh watched her slip her fingers beneath his waistband, then gently ease the cotton over him and down his legs to join the pile of discarded clothing on the floor.

Reaching out, she ran one gentle fingertip down the length of his penis. His erection jerked, and a moan rushed past his lips. Before he could regroup, she leaned forward and licked him.

And he sure as hell melted.

Gritting his teeth against the intense pleasure, he watched her run her tongue over him, licking, tasting, kissing the full length of him, while her hands caressed and cupped him. Just when he didn't think he could take any more, she took him into her wet mouth.

A groan ripped from his chest. Her tongue slowly circled him and his entire body tightened. Sweat dampened his skin, and the need to come pounded through him with increasing desperation. He wasn't going to be able to hold off his orgasm much longer. And the hell with not touching her.

Tunneling shaking fingers through her hair, he withstood the sweet torture of her mouth for another half a minute. "Lexie." Her name was a long, hunger-filled growl. She slowly released him from her mouth, but gave him no time to catch his breath. Still straddling his legs, she leaned forward and pulled a condom from beneath the pillow. Within seconds the condom was on, her panties were off, and his erection was buried deep in her tight wet, heat.

He tried to slow down, to retain some modicum of control, but his control was long gone. Reaching under her dress, he grasped her hips and thrust upward hard and fast.

"Josh..." Hearing her moan his name in that harsh, needful voice, pushed him over the edge. His release pounded through him with an intensity that bordered on pain. He throbbed inside her, shudders racking him, absorbing the feel of her orgasm as she pulsed around him. When his spasms subsided, he lay beneath her, ragged breaths pumping from his lungs, a film of sweat covering his skin, his heart beating so hard and fast he could hear its echo in his head.

He wasn't sure how long it took him to recover enough to force his eyes open. When he did, he discovered her looking down at him with the same stunned expression he knew had to be on his face.

Still intimately joined, they shared a long, silent look. Love, sure and strong, rushed through him, filling him with the certainty that it was only a matter of time before she realized that this was not a fling. Reaching up, he grasped her arms and pulled her down to him for an intimate, openmouthed kiss. Then she propped her weight on her hands and pulled back, looking at him with hazel eyes that glowed with a wicked gleam.

"So...did you melt?"

"Honey, you absolutely liquefied me. There's nothin' solid left."

"Oh. That's too bad. I wasn't nearly done with you."

"Yeah, well, I haven't even gotten started with you." His gaze shifted over her dress and he shook his head. "Didn't even get all your clothes off."

"No, but I kinda liked that you were naked and I wasn't. Of course, that does go against your cowboy rule about clothes in the bedroom being a waste of time. Did you mind?"

"Not a bit. But just remember, turnaround is fair play."

"Hmm. Is that a threat?"

"It's a promise."

"You know where else clothes are a waste of time?" she asked, lightly kissing him between each word. "The hot tub."

"Anything in that water that might bite me on the ass?"

A devilish grin eased over her face. "Only me."

"Good thing I'm now fearless in the water."

"How fearless?"

"I'd be happy to show you."

7

LEXIE AWOKE to the sound of birds chirping and bright sunlight filtering through the partially opened blinds. Memories of last night flooded into her mind, and she stretched sinuously, enjoying the pleasurable ache in her muscles. She turned to greet Josh, but discovered herself alone.

Rising, she slipped on her short, pale blue satin robe, noting as she tied the sash around her waist that Josh's clothes were no longer on the floor. She padded down the hallway and sighed in appreciation when the scent of fresh-brewed coffee wafted toward her from the kitchen. She entered the room, a smile on her lips, but Josh wasn't there. Instead she discovered a note printed on a napkin next to the coffeemaker. She quickly scanned the words.

Good morning, Sleepyhead,
Your cupboard was sort of bare, and for reasons that are entirely your fault, I'm in need of a sub-stantial breakfast. Be back soon with the grub.

Josh

She grinned at the big smiley face he'd drawn next to his name, then poured herself a much-needed cup of coffee. Opening the sliding patio door, she stepped out onto the deck. She loved to spend the mornings on her days off out here, sitting on the comfy green-and-peach-striped lounger, drinking coffee and perusing the newspaper. After settling herself, she enjoyed her first sip as her gaze zeroed in on the hot tub.

A wealth of sensual memories ambushed her and she expelled a long, satisfied sigh. Holy cow. Last night had been…amazing. Even more so than the previous night. Yet more than just amazing. Because they'd shared so much more than just physical intimacy. She and Josh had talked and laughed and joked. Shared childhood and work-related anecdotes. Fed each other popcorn during their hot-tub soak. They'd had fun together. Which was great since *fun* was rule number one for a fling.

It had been a long time since she'd thought of lovemaking as fun. While she'd enjoyed her physical relationship with Tony, he wasn't one to talk much before, during or after. Josh, on the other hand, had no qualms about asking if he was pleasing her and telling her what pleased him. And he wasn't afraid to laugh, as he had when, during a passionate kiss in the hot tub, her cat Scout had jumped up onto the ledge and interrupted them by meowing loudly next to Josh's ear.

And while sex with Tony had been good, sex with Josh was…incredible. There was a chemistry between them that she'd never experienced before. An intimacy and spark that simultaneously thrilled and frightened her. Thrilled her because she'd clearly chosen the perfect lover with whom to indulge in a fling. And frightened her because it was growing increasingly difficult to ignore the little voice in her head that kept saying, *If you think this is just sex, you're an idiot. You're speeding straight toward a head-on collision with heartbreak.*

Her eyes slid closed and she blew out a sigh. Damn

that annoying little voice. Why couldn't it just shut up and let her have some fun?

I won't shut up because I'm right. And in your heart, you know it.

Another sigh. How could she deny it? She liked Josh. A lot. It was one thing to like a fling-guy *in* bed, but she liked him just as much *out* of bed. And the more time she spent with him—both in and out of bed—the more she liked him. In an unwanted, ever-increasing way that could indeed lead to heartbreak. But she couldn't seem to put the brakes on her feelings. It didn't matter that she repeatedly reminded herself that he lived and owned a ranch thousands of miles away from Florida— her home that she had no intention of leaving.

And even if, by some geographical miracle, Montana and Florida were only minutes apart, there was no getting around the fact that Josh was, by no stretch of the imagination, the non-danger-loving accountant/insurance-salesman type. Good grief, he'd spent half his life getting tossed off the backs of huge bucking beasts! And now, here he was, his mind set on conquering the seven seas with a gritty-eyed determination she recognized all too well, thanks to Tony.

"He's my transition man," she muttered. "Nothing more. Fun, wild and *temporary.*"

Yeah, right, her inner voice snickered.

Well, he was. And if it weren't for the fact that she needed the extra money he was paying her for lessons, she'd tell him to get lost. Take a hike.

Yeah, right.

"Good morning," came Josh's deep voice from the patio doorway. "Napping already?"

Opening her eyes, her heart skipped a beat at the sight of him. Freshly shaved and dressed in a snowy

T-shirt and snug jeans faded in all the right places, he looked big and tall and lean and good enough to lick. Again.

Smiling she said, "Good morning. Not napping. Just lounging and enjoying the morning sun."

He crossed the deck then sat on the edge of her lounge chair. Leaning down, he kissed her with a lingering, gentle perfection that stole her breath. When he lifted his head, she felt so drugged, she had to struggle to lift her eyelids. "Wow," she whispered. "You're really good at that."

Her heart stuttered at the compelling expression in his dark eyes. "So are you." He brushed his fingers over her lips. "You have the most beautiful mouth I've ever seen. I can't tell you how much sleep I've lost since I met you, fantasizing about that mouth."

He looked so serious, she felt the need to lighten the mood—before she blurted out something inappropriate and stupid like, *You're the most beautiful man I've ever seen and I think I'm falling head over heels for you.* Clearing her throat, she forced what she hoped passed for a sexy, lighthearted smile. "Well, my mouth made you lose some sleep *last* night."

"Honey, your mouth about stopped my heart last night." He picked up her hand and brought it to his lips, pressing a kiss into her palm. "In fact, the entire night about stopped my heart."

His warm breath drifted over her skin, and the intense, almost troubled expression in his eyes stilled her. Was he feeling it, too? This unsettling, growing unease that their fling could turn into something more?

She was spared the need to reply, just as well as it seemed someone had tied a big knot in her tongue, when he appeared to shake off his seriousness and smiled. "I stopped at the resort to change and pick up a few things for our sailing lesson. Then I hit the grocery store. No offense, but the contents of your refrigerator looked like a food museum."

Embarrassment heated her face. "Sorry. Free meals are one of the perks of working at the resort, so I don't keep much on hand here. I usually shop on my day off, which is today. It's on my list of things to do."

"Well, cross it off your list 'cause it's done. I bought bacon, eggs, muffins, pancake mix, syrup—all the fixin's for a hearty country breakfast." Her dismay must have shown because he asked, "That okay?"

"It's fine. It's just that...well, I'm afraid I'm not that great in the kitchen. Pouring a bowl of cereal is about as fancy as I get for breakfast. I suppose I could scorch some toast if I really *had* to."

"You don't cook?"

Humph. Obviously he didn't feel that pouring cereal and scorching toast fell into the realm of "cooking." Well, too bad. "I'm sort of the anti-cook."

He rose and pulled her to her feet. Taking her into his arms, he dropped a quick kiss on her nose. "Lucky for you, I'm a great cook."

She squeezed her eyes shut. No. Impossible. He simply could not be gorgeous, funny, charming, nice, sexy, *and* know how to cook. "You're joking."

"Darlin', I might kid about a lot of things, but food preparation is not one of them. Cowboys take their grub very seriously." He started toward the kitchen, tugging lightly on her hand. "C'mon. I'll make you a breakfast guaranteed to knock your socks off."

She followed him into the kitchen, shaking her head. Great. Just what she needed—another reason to like him.

And damn it, he'd already knocked a heck of a lot more than her socks off.

JOSH LEANED BACK in the comfortable kitchen chair. Over the rim of his yellow ceramic coffee mug, he watched Lexie finish her last bite of pancake, her eyes closed in rapture, a purr of satisfaction rumbling in her throat. If there was one thing he liked, it was a woman who enjoyed food. And he'd never met one who looked more decadent and downright sexy while she ate than Lexie.

"That was, by far, the best breakfast I've eaten in a long time," she said, tapping her napkin against her lips. "Definitely beats cold cereal."

"Glad you enjoyed it. But I thought you got free meals at the resort."

"I do. But I usually eat a light breakfast. Fruit, maybe a muffin. I don't have much time in the morning before the early activities start. Besides, big meals make me sleepy."

"Great! Wanna go to bed?" He waggled his brows in an exaggerated leer.

She laughed, then batted her eyelashes in an equally outrageous fashion. "Why, Mr. Maynard. Are you trying to seduce me?"

"Every chance I get." He glanced down at his watch and shook his head with genuine regret. "Except right now. It's getting late. There's just enough time for me to clean up the dishes while you get dressed. Wear comfortable jeans."

She raised her brows. "Jeans? For sailing?"

"No, jeans for your surprise. We can start the sailing lessons later this afternoon."

"Surprise? What surprise?"

"Now if I told you that, it wouldn't be a surprise."

Leaning toward her, he allowed himself a quick taste of her sweet mouth, then rose before he gave in to temptation and chucked all his fine plans for the rest of the morning. Rising, he carried their dirty dishes to the sink, then turned on the faucet.

She followed him, peering into the sink. "Don't tell me you wash dishes, too."

"Well, only if they don't fit in the dishwasher."

She swiveled her head to look at him. "You load the dishwasher?"

"Unless you've got dishes that know how to hop in there all by themselves." He gave her a gentle swat on the butt. "Go get dressed so we're not late."

"Will you give me a hint what this surprise is?"

"Only that you're gonna love it." He laughed at her skeptical look. "I promise."

"WHAT THE HELL is that?"

Lexie looked at the huge beast eyeballing her with unmistakable suspicion and experienced a sensation that felt unpleasantly like an all-over body cramp. Oh, boy. She had a real bad feeling about this.

"*That* is a horse," Josh said with a smile, running his hand over the animal's glossy brown neck. A teenage boy stood next to the animal, holding the reins. "And I'm going to teach you how to ride her."

"Like hell." Sweat popped out on her brow. "Look, Josh, remember how I told you I'd never been on a horse? Well, that's not exactly accurate. I tried riding. Once. I was eight. I spent thirty seconds on the horse, ten seconds sailing through the air, then six weeks with a cast on my broken arm."

Understanding dawned in his eyes. "You were thrown. And you've been afraid of horses ever since."

The horse pawed at the ground and breathed out a loud snort. Lexie took two hasty steps backward and nodded. "That's it in a nutshell, yup."

"Sort of like the way I got bit on the ass by that snake and never learned to swim."

"I suppose," she admitted grudgingly. "But unlike you, I suffer from B.F.C. Syndrome, a condition that makes it impossible for me to get on a horse."

Instant concern clouded his eyes. "B.F.C. Syndrome? What is that? Some sort of allergy?"

"Big Fat Chicken Syndrome. I'm afraid my case is fatal."

He looked heavenward, muttered something under his breath that sounded suspiciously like, "Women! Can't live with 'em, can't kill 'em," then erased the several yards between them. Resting his hands on her shoulders he said, "You taught me what you're good at. Let me teach you what I'm good at."

"I thought what you were good at was getting tossed off the back of bucking Brahman bulls. No thanks."

"Actually, what I was good at was *staying on* the back of bucking Brahman bulls. This is not a bull. It's a horse. A very sweet, gentle, docile horse."

Her gaze alternated between his earnest face and the horse, who, she had to admit, appeared pretty docile. At the moment. "What's its name?"

He pinched the bridge of his nose and shook his head as if in pain. "Believe it or not, somebody named this gorgeous animal…Yogurt."

The horse tossed its head and snorted. Josh nodded in clear commiseration. "I know, baby. I feel your pain with that one." He shook his head again, muttering, "Yogurt. Good God."

"Well, that settles it," Lexie said. "I cannot possibly ride a horse named Yogurt."

"Why not?"

"I'm lactose intolerant."

A tiny smile twitched his lips. "If *I* can bring myself to ride a horse named Yogurt, so can you."

"That's the problem. I can't ride a horse by *any* name. You can. You're a cowboy. You could ride a horse named Bone Crusher." She took a few more steps backward. "Besides, you're brave. I'm a—"

"B.F.C.?"

She narrowed her eyes at him. "Are you calling me fat?"

He settled his hands on his hips, looking skyward. "No. And don't think I don't recognize one of those 'girl trap' questions when I hear one." Taking her hands, he gave them what she was certain he meant as a reassuring squeeze.

"Lexie. You're nervous. I understand. But if I didn't honestly think you would love this, if I didn't know you'd be perfectly safe, I wouldn't ask you to try it. Remember what you told me during our first lesson, about how having an experienced instructor will give you the confidence to overcome your fears? Give it five minutes. Give *me* five minutes. Let me show you how exhilarating riding can be. I'll be sitting right behind you, my arms around you. I swear I won't let anything happen to you. If, after five minutes, you hate it, we'll stop."

Looking up into his handsome, earnest face, her heart performed a slow somersault. How could she possibly refuse him? Besides, with Josh right behind her, his strong arms around her, she'd probably forget she was even *on* a horse. Probably.

Disgusted for feeling like such a total wimp, but unable to stop the question, she asked, "You won't let go of me?"

"I won't let go of you," he promised softly, his eyes filled with an expression that stalled her breath.

Swallowing hard, she summoned her courage, then jerked her head in a nod. "All right. I guess I can stand anything for five minutes."

A huge smile lit his face. "Sweetheart, you're about to have the best five minutes of your life. So good you won't want to stop."

Holding tightly on to his hand, she allowed him to lead her back to Yogurt. Yeah, she could believe that five minutes wrapped in Josh's arms could win the Best Five Minutes of her life award. She just prayed these weren't about to be her *last* five minutes.

An hour later, Lexie leaned back against Josh's hard chest. With the back of her head resting against his shoulder, she tipped her face up to the sun, closed her eyes, and enjoyed the warming rays filtering through the palm trees against her skin. The only sounds were the chirping birds, the rustling leaves, and the squeak of the leather saddle as they moved slowly along the shady path.

But the sun wasn't solely responsible for the almost drugging warmth seeping through her. No, that sensation was caused by Josh. His body touching the entire length of hers. Her back to his chest. Her hips and thighs nestled snugly by his. His strong, sinewy, golden-brown forearms cradling hers. His calloused palms and fingers wrapped around hers on the leather reins.

He surrounded her like a down-filled quilt on a chilly night, infusing her with warmth and security and comfort. His heartbeat thumped against her shoulder, his chin bumped her temple with Yogurt's gently swaying gait. With him holding her like this, her nervousness hadn't lasted long. And indeed, at the end of those first five minutes, all she'd wanted was to feel more. More of sharing this experience with him. More of him showing her the proper way to hold the reins. More of feeling him pressed intimately against her back, his clean, masculine scent all around her. *Him* all around her.

His lips brushed against her temple. "You okay?" His warm breath caressed her cheek.

"Very okay." Turning her head, she lightly kissed his jaw. "So okay that I hereby give you permission to say it."

He didn't pretend to misunderstand, and chuckled. "I told you so."

His deep voice vibrated against her, adding another layer of warmth. Opening her eyes, she noted a flash of deep turquoise between the trees. "This path leads to the water?"

"It does. It's the reason I chose this place for your lesson. They own a stretch of private beach we can ride on. I figured you'd like that."

"How did you even know about this place? And that they owned a stretch of beach?"

"Two wonderful little inventions called the telephone and the Yellow Pages."

Surprise and pleasure washed over her at the fact that he'd gone to such trouble to arrange this outing, and not just at any stable, but one by the beach. For her.

They rounded a corner and suddenly sparkling aqua water and bright white sand stretched in front of them. "You know," he said, "I practically grew up in the saddle, but I've never ridden on a beach before."

Straightening, she smiled at him over her shoulder. "So in a way, this is a first for you, too."

He didn't return her smile. He just studied her for several long seconds with an unreadable expression. She couldn't look away from him, and her smile slowly faded, her heart thumping hard under the weight of his serious regard. Finally he said, his voice low and husky, "Yeah. This is a first for me."

Heat pulsed through her. Heat that had nothing, yet everything, to do with his nearness, his quiet dark eyes, his compelling voice. Leaning forward, he whispered in her ear, "Hang on, sweetheart. Here comes the next best five minutes of your life."

Lexie wasn't sure how it happened, but one second they were standing still, and the next they were racing across the sand, wind whipping her hair into chaos, exhilaration stealing her breath. Safe and secure in Josh's strong arms, they galloped along the shoreline, Yogurt's flashing hooves kicking up sprays of water.

She savored every second of the experience, all of her senses vibrantly alive. The strength of the man behind her and the horse beneath her. The ribbons of golden sunshine reflecting on the azure water, in sharp contrast to the stark white sand. The scent of horse and leather and tropical heat and Josh. The beach was deserted, a pristine sanctuary just for them to share.

As they neared a sign indicating the end of the stable's private beach, he slowed Yogurt down to a walk, then finally halted her. "Well?" he breathed into Lexie's ear.

"Incredible. Exhilarating. Exciting." Turning her head, she pressed a breathless kiss to his chin. Then, slipping her hands from beneath his, she spread her arms, encompassing their tropical surroundings. "Isn't this view terrific? I love the water. Someday I'm going to live right on the water."

He wrapped one strong arm around her, resting his chin on her shoulder. "Right *on* the water? Won't that be a little damp?"

She laughed. "I mean, waterfront property." She pointed across the glimmering strip of azure water. "Like over there. See that group of houses? That's a new development. Just to the right of them is some great waterfront property. A whole series of canals and hidden coves. It's peaceful and private and perfect." And someday she would own her piece of it...the piece she'd wanted since the first moment she'd seen it. The only things standing between her and that dream was the wait for the owner to sell, and a big pile of money. All she needed was the down payment. Hopefully, when the time came, she'd have enough.

His arm tightened around her. "Looks nice. Sounds nice, too."

Turning her head so she could see his eyes, she said, "Thank you, Josh, for a wonderful, thoughtful surprise. And for bringing me here. It's beautiful."

"Yeah," he murmured, his gaze roaming her face before settling on her lips. "Sure is beautiful."

She lifted her face, intending to give him a brief kiss, but the instant their lips met, the kiss turned hot, wet and demanding. His tongue explored her mouth with a hunger that heated her from the inside out. A long moan purred in Lexie's throat and she wished their position were less awkward so she could touch more of him.

With his mouth insistent on hers, he flicked open the top three buttons of her sleeveless cotton blouse, then caressed the tops of her breasts with one hand, while the other continued down to rest low on her belly.

Breaking off their kiss, he ran his lips across her throat while she raised her arms over her head then back to encircle his neck. His strong, warm fingers slipped beneath the lace of her bra to tease her aroused nipples, while his other hand lightly traced intoxicating circles between her spread legs straddling the saddle. His erection pressed against her buttocks, and she arched back, rubbing herself against him.

"Lexie." He breathed her name in a passionate whisper against her overheated skin, a whisper that ended in a groan of masculine longing. "Let's go home. Now."

"What was that you said to me the other night?" she whispered. "Oh, yes. Great minds think alike."

JOSH SPENT the thirty-minute-drive back to Lexie's house trying to corral the need raging through him. Damn it, he'd never felt so unsettled in his life. Or impatient to get his hands on a woman's skin. Feel her. Taste her. Have her wrapped all around him.

This loving a woman was a real pain in the ass. Why the hell couldn't he just have fallen in *lust* with her? Lust he knew and understood. But noo-ooo. He had to fall in love with a woman who only wanted a fling. He felt as though he was picking his way through an emotional minefield and that any second he was going to get blown to bits. But there was no way in hell he could consider retreat.

By the time he pulled into her driveway and cut the

engine, he had himself and the need clawing at him back under control. In fact, he congratulated himself on his restraint. All the way into the foyer.

He watched her lock the door behind them, and in the blink of an eye, all bets were off. The instant she'd turned the bolt into place, he turned her around and kissed her with all the pent-up need he foolishly thought he'd pushed back. He stepped forward, pinning her against the door with his body, and yanked her shirt out of her jeans with one hand, while the other impatiently worked the buttons free. Seconds later he parted the white cotton and settled his hands on her warm, bare stomach.

But the feel of her skin beneath his hands brought him no relief, only fueled his need. His inner voice told him to slow down, but it was impossible. Not with her hands splayed on his ass, pressing him closer, grinding herself against him.

He pushed her blouse down her arms, then unclasped her bra. Both fell to the tiled floor. Breaking their frantic kiss, he took her tight nipple into his mouth, absorbing her sharp gasp. It was all he could do not to take her right against the door, but some drop of sanity prevailed. They needed a condom, and the damn things were in the bedroom. And there was no way he was leaving her here while he went to get one.

Dipping his knees, he lifted her up. She instantly wrapped her legs around his waist, and with her showering his face and neck with hot kisses, he managed, somehow, to get them to the bedroom, making a mental vow to never come near this woman again without a condom in his pocket.

He deposited her in the center of the mattress with a gentle bounce, then immediately moved to the nightstand where he grabbed a condom from the box he'd brought with him and stashed there before their riding lesson. It took him of all ten seconds to return to her, and in that time she'd managed to divest herself of her shoes and socks, and was applying herself to her jeans.

Without a word, their gazes fused, she shimmied out of her snug denim and panties, while he unfastened his jeans. He couldn't get them off without stopping to remove his boots, and that was simply out of the question. He needed to be inside her *now*.

Pushing his Levi's and boxers down to his hips, he rolled on the condom, gritting his teeth against the unbearably arousing sight of her lying naked on her aqua comforter, legs splayed, nipples wet and erect from his mouth, eyes smoky with want.

An inferno roared through him, taking him over. Helpless to stop it, he thrust into her, all fire and incinerating heat. Gentleness was beyond him. But she met him all the way, wrapping her legs around him, urging him with desperate whispers to go faster. Harder.

He tried to hold off his orgasm, but it was like trying to hold back the ocean with a broom. Seconds later his release pounded through him, pulling a growl from his throat. Clutching her to him, he buried his face in the fragrant curve of her neck.

He lay there, panting, sweating, heart hammering, unable to move. He remained inside her, her limbs wrapped around him, listening to her rapid breaths battering against his ear. He wasn't sure how long it took for reason to return. When it finally did, he lifted his head. And looked down into gold-flecked hazel eyes glowing up at him.

"Holy cow," she whispered. A short laugh puffed

between her parted lips. "How many times can we do that before we both pass out?"

"I don't know. What's the record?"

That brought a smile. "I'm not sure how it's possible to feel half dead and fantastic at the same time, but you've managed to make that happen."

"Glad to know I didn't leave you hangin' at the starting gate. I didn't mean to come so soon. Couldn't stop it."

"Don't be sorry on my account. Your timing was perfect." Raising her arms above her head, she stretched with abandon. "I guess turnaround *is* fair play. This time I'm the one without the clothes."

"I would've exploded if I'd taken the time to undress."

An unmistakable feminine gleam glittered in her eyes. "Hmm. I insist you tell me what I did to inspire such passion so I can make sure I do it again. As soon as possible."

A frown pulled at Josh's brow. What *had* she done to make him lose control like that? To rob him of his finesse in that unprecedented way? To make him want her with a desperation that he'd never felt for another woman? The answer hit with the force of a sucker punch.

That's what love did to a man. She'd done nothing except *be* with him. She'd laughed with him. Talked to him. Looked at him with those big, expressive eyes. Shared a ride on the beach with him. Then thanked him for the experience. She'd seduced him, without even trying, simply by being herself, and she'd done it long before she'd actually kissed him. And he'd kissed her with such raw need and hunger because he'd already been thoroughly seduced. Because he loved her.

How the hell could he possibly hope to explain that to her without telling her truths he sensed she wasn't ready to hear? Truths that if he revealed too soon he feared might make her bolt like a spooked rabbit? Hell, except for Lexie, if a woman he'd just met a few days ago had told him she loved him, he'd have disappeared so fast he would have left a vapor trail behind him.

He wanted to tell her how he felt about her, but damn it, he was afraid. Afraid it was too soon. Afraid she'd tell him to get lost. Afraid she wouldn't love him back.

A bomb exploded in the emotional minefield he was trying, with little success, to navigate. As much as he might not want to, he needed to wait a little longer before he threw his heart into the arena.

Luckily he was spared the need to respond when Scout jumped onto the bed and let loose with a loud meow.

"She's saying hello," Lexie said with a smile.

Josh winked at the cat who, he swore, winked back.

"She responds well to flattery," Lexie said.

Flattery? "Er, cats rule, dogs drool."

Scout clearly agreed. After an extensive butt-in-the-air stretch, she curled up on Lexie's pillow with a contented purr, then shut her eyes.

Not anxious to return to her unanswered question about how she'd inspired such passion in him, Josh asked, "Why'd you name her Scout?"

"The day I brought her home from the animal shelter, she climbed out of her sleeping box. I found her curled up in my bookcase. She was so tiny and cute, snoozing away on my copy of *To Kill a Mockingbird*."

"She probably thought it was a feline how-to manual."

Lexie laughed. "Probably. So I named her after Scout in the book." She wriggled a bit, arousing interest in body parts he'd thought would have been unrousable for quite some time yet.

"I didn't think I'd ever say this after that huge breakfast you made, but I think I'm hungry again."

"It's all that fresh air and exercise." He brushed a wayward curl from her forehead. "Just to warn you, you'll probably be pretty sore tomorrow from our ride."

Mischief danced in her eyes. "Our *horseback* ride?"

"That would be the one."

"I'll be fine. I'm in good shape."

"You sure are." He dropped a quick kiss on her tempting lips. "I vote we grab some lunch, then start our first sailing lesson."

"Sounds great." Her smile warmed him down to his boots. "You're going to love sailing."

"I guess I can stand anything for five minutes," he teased, echoing her earlier words before their ride.

"It will be the best five minutes of your life. So good you won't want to stop."

He looked into her eyes and another bomb in the minefield detonated.

Suddenly he didn't doubt her words for a minute.

And that scared the hell out of him.

8

BY FOUR O'CLOCK that afternoon Josh had realized several things. First, he was very glad he'd read extensively on the subject of sailing before coming to Florida, because it enabled him to move swiftly through Lexie's thorough textbook-type preliminaries on topics such as types of boats and sails, how sailboats work, and a slew of nautical terms. His knowledge also came with the extra bonus that it impressed his teacher. Especially his knot-tying skills. "I'm pretty handy with a rope," he said with a smile. "Comes with the cowboy territory."

Second, it was obvious, even more so than during their swimming lessons, that Lexie was an excellent teacher. Patient, encouraging, knowledgeable and thorough, she explained things in a clear, concise manner, always emphasizing safety. She took their lesson seriously, and took him seriously, as well. Yet in spite of her seriousness her sense of humor shone through, making the lesson fun as well as informative. They spent three hours sitting at her kitchen table doing classroom legwork before driving back to the Whispering Palms to actually sail one of the resort's rental boats.

And third, as the afternoon flew by, Josh realized that it was possible to fall even deeper in love with a woman he was already completely in love with.

While he sat at that kitchen table, his mind engaged in learning about mainsails, masts, transoms, beams, keels, tacks, booms and the rest of it, his heart was getting blown to further bits in the minefield.

She appealed to him on every level: physical, emotional, intellectual and everywhere in between. He didn't just love her—he genuinely *liked* her. And he knew it wouldn't be long before he'd have to tell her how he felt.

Damn it, he hadn't wanted or planned for this complication, and wasn't particularly pleased about the kink meeting her had thrown into all his finely laid-out plans, but there was no way he could consider ignoring how he felt. Yup, unfortunately this situation was not like passing a dead skunk on the road—he couldn't just roll up the windows and keep on going. He wanted, needed, to know if she felt any of these same overwhelming emotions.

And as soon as this sailing lesson was over, he was going to find out.

THEIR LESSON ENDED at 6:00 p.m. and just as his teacher had predicted, Josh had enjoyed every minute of it. The cool spray of water, the concentration and challenge required to handle the sixteen-foot craft, Lexie's patient instructions as he got the feel of the boat, and mostly Lexie's company.

After returning the boat to the rental dock, they walked back toward the main area of the resort along a foliage-lined cement path that meandered along the perimeter of the property.

Taking her hand, he squeezed her fingers. She squeezed back, looking up at him with a dazzling smile that shot a tingle straight through him. "You did great," she said. "You caught on faster than any student I've ever had. You're a natural."

Lifting her hand, he placed a kiss on the inside of her wrist, noting with pleasure that her eyes darkened at the gesture. "A student's progress is a direct reflection of the teacher, and I picked a winner."

"Well, as much as I'd like to take all the credit, I can't. You were able to 'feel' the boat, the way it reacted to the wind and the water, with an ability few beginners possess. And you were calm. Relaxed. Focused. You wouldn't believe how many people are tense and panicky. Plus, you're good with the ropes—" she laughed. "There's a lot of ropes in sailing. And you have good sailing hands. Strong and steady."

He waggled his brows. "You tryin' to tell me I'm good with my hands, Miss Lexie?"

Color rushed into her cheeks, utterly charming him. "Are we still talking about sailing?"

"You tell me."

"All right. You are *very* good with your hands. On the boat, and off."

An image of his hands caressing her soft skin flashed in his mind, hiking his temperature up a notch, but since he had no desire to walk around the still populated pool area with an erection, he forced his mind to other matters. "Are you hungry?"

She waggled her brows at him this time. "Are you talking about food?"

"For starters." He patted his stomach with his free hand. "Lunch is loo-oong gone. May I take you to dinner?"

"That sounds great. Do you want to eat here?"

He shook his head. "Actually I already made reservations somewhere else."

She raised her brows. "You did? What if I'd said no?"

"I would have done my best to change your mind."

"Hmm. Maybe I should have said no," she teased. "Where did you make reservations?"

"The Blue Flamingo."

Her eyes widened. "That's my favorite restaurant!"

"I know."

She pursed her lips. "I don't recall mentioning that."

"You didn't. When I came back here for my things this morning, I spoke to Maurice at the concierge desk. Real nice fella. Wife just had a baby. Anyway, I told him I wanted to ask you to dinner and could he recommend a good place. When he mentioned the Blue Flamingo was your favorite, I asked him to make reservations for us. Think you can be ready by eight?"

"Yes, but I'm afraid you'll need to drive me home. I only keep a basic change of clothes here in the employee locker room—certainly nothing nice enough for the Blue Flamingo."

He stopped, then pulled her slowly into his arms. "Are you telling me that you don't have anything to wear? 'Cause to me, that sounds like *good* news."

She narrowed her eyes at him. "Hey. You're not trying to renege on your invite are you?"

"Absolutely not." He gently rubbed himself against her. "In fact, the thought of you having nothing to wear inspires me to issue another invitation." He whispered a suggestion in her ear.

Leaning back in the circle of his arms, she regarded him with wide eyes. "Wow. Is that even anatomically possible?"

"I don't know. Wanna take a quick detour up to my room and find out?"

A slow smile lit her face. "Like you wouldn't believe."

LEXIE STOOD in her shower, the warm spray pelting her skin. Josh would be back in less than an hour to pick her up for dinner. A smile played around her lips at his insistence on bringing her home, then returning to his hotel room to change, then driving back to pick her up "like a real date." Not that a ton of driving was involved—her house was only minutes from the resort, but his chivalry touched a feminine instinct in her she'd thought long dead. It certainly wasn't a gesture Tony ever would have thought to make. In fact, she couldn't recall Tony ever saying anything even remotely like, "Dress up, we're going out on the town." No, Tony's invitations were normally accompanied by instructions like, "Hold on tight" and "Don't worry, the parachute will open."

Turning off the water, she wrapped a towel around herself sarong-style. Anticipation filled her at dining at the Blue Flamingo. She only ate at the elegant five-star restaurant on very special occasions as the prices majorly strained the budget. The food, the service, the atmosphere, the small dance floor, all made for a fabulous dining experience.

Oh, sure. The food and the service—that's why you can't wait to go, her inner voice piped up as she towel-dried her hair. *Doesn't have anything to do with the man taking you there.*

Wiping the steam from the mirror, Lexie stared at her reflection. After a good, long, hard look, she shook her head. Who was she trying to fool? Damn it, she was practically glowing. All but twinkling, for crying out loud. And it had nothing to do with the prospect of the Blue Flamingo's lobster thermidor.

Leaning closer to the mirror she said, "Josh is taking you to the diner for a burger and fries."

Glow and twinkle remained in place.

"Dinner with Josh is going to consist of stale bread and warm water."

Glow and twinkle.

"Josh is catching the next flight back to Manhattan, Montana, and you'll never see him again."

Glow and twinkle snuffed out like a candle in a hurricane.

Oh, boy. This was not good.

The phone rang and she gratefully exited the bathroom with its all-too-knowing mirror. Grabbing the portable receiver from her nightstand she said, "Hello?"

"Lexie, it's Darla. Is this a bad time? Am I—" her voice dropped to a whisper "—*interrupting* anything?"

Lexie laughed. "No. I'd hardly pick up the phone if you were."

"Is the cowboy there?"

"No, but he's picking me up soon and I'm not ready yet. What's up?"

"That's what I'm calling to ask you. How's everything going? Still keeping things in perspective?"

Glow and twinkle. Glow and twinkle. "Uh, yeah."

"Uh-oh. I know that tone. Sounds to me like you need another pep talk."

Lexie heaved out a sigh. "I think I might." *A big pep talk.*

"Well, never fear, Darla is here. How about breakfast tomorrow?"

"Can't. I'm giving an early lesson. How about lunch? Noon at the Marine Patio?"

"Done. Now go and make yourself gorgeous for your evening with Mr. Cowboy. What are you guys doing—as if I need to ask?"

"He's taking me to the Blue Flamingo."

A soft whistle came through the receiver. "Very nice. Well, you kids have a great time, and don't do anything I wouldn't do."

"So the sky's the limit, huh?" Lexie teased.

"You got it, babe. Now, repeat after me. This is just a fling."

Taking a deep breath, Lexie said, "This is just a fling." The words tasted like sawdust on her tongue.

"Good girl. Go out, have a great time, and just repeat those words as necessary until I see you tomorrow."

They exchanged goodbyes and Lexie set down the receiver. Then, straightening her shoulders, she headed toward her closet, muttering for all she was worth, "This is just a fling."

FORTY-FIVE MINUTES later, Lexie opened her front door and every thought and mutter drained from her head.

Holy cow. He'd looked sublime in jeans and a T-shirt. Fabulous in a swimsuit. Incredible in his birthday suit. But here he stood wearing a dark blue, pinstriped business suit and a snowy-white shirt bisected by a red, paisley-print silk tie, and damn near stopped her heart. *Somebody call the cops—I've been robbed. This guy has swiped my ability to breathe. And bring the paramedics while you're at it in case I go into cardiac arrest.*

Her gaze wandered up and down his scrumptious length, noting his tasteful black tassel loafers and the single long-stemmed red rose he held, before returning to his face.

He smiled at her and extended the rose. "Hi."

"H-hi." Yikes. Was that croaky whisper her voice? Reaching out a none-too-steady hand, she accepted the flower. Breathing in its heady fragrance, she watched his eyes skim over her in that appreciative way that brought goose bumps to her skin.

"I didn't know cowboys wore suits," she said in that same croaky voice.

"Only when we're off the ranch. Even bull riders like to put on the dog every once in a while."

"Well, you put it on *very* well."

"Glad you approve. I actually brought the fancy duds to meet with one of my corporate sponsors next week, but I'd much rather wear it for you." He finished his perusal of her and their eyes met. "You look beautiful, Lexie."

Josh stood on her porch and tried not to stare with his mouth hanging open, but it was damn near impossible. The way her black dress left her golden shoulders bare, how the full skirt hugged her hips and danced just above her knees, and those sexy, strappy heels that made her legs appear endless...whew.

That feminine, flowery scent she wore that drove him nuts wafted off her smooth skin, beckoning him to bury his face in the delicate hollow of her collarbone. How the hell was he going to keep his hands off her all during dinner? Maybe they could just order their meal to go. Unfortunately, he doubted the Blue Flamingo had a drive-thru window.

"Come on in," she said, rousing him from his stupor. He entered the foyer, pulling a deep, calming breath into his lungs. He'd be fine in just a second. Just needed some air.

"Can I get you something before we leave? A drink maybe?" She closed the door, then smiled—a shy sort of smile that certainly shouldn't have speeded up his pulse.

"How about a kiss?"

"That can be arranged," she murmured, stepping closer and lifting her face.

He brushed his mouth over hers, forcing himself to keep the contact light, knowing if he didn't they'd never get out of the foyer with their clothes intact.

When he lifted his head she said softly, her warm breath touching his face, "Thank you for the rose. It's lovely."

"*You're* lovely." He touched one fingertip to her soft cheek. "Looks like you got a little sun today."

"Actually, I think that's more likely a postcoital glow—and completely your fault."

He hardened instantly as images of their earlier heated lovemaking flashed through his mind...images he needed to banish, at least temporarily, if they had a prayer of getting to the restaurant.

Taking her resolutely by the shoulders—and absolutely not noticing how satiny her skin felt beneath his hands—he urged her toward the kitchen. "I'll wait here while you put your rose in water," he said, inwardly cringing at the note of desperation in his voice. "Then we can go."

"Okay. Be right back," she said, then turned toward the kitchen.

The relieved breath he was about to suck into his lungs stalled in his throat as he watched her walk away. Her dress left her entire back bare, from her shoulders to her waist. Nothing but smooth skin, and lots of it, begging for a man to caress.

Damn. She looked like walking, breathing sin in that dress.

He couldn't wait to get it off her.

He just prayed his heart could stand the wait.

"WOULD YOU LIKE to dance, Lexie?"

The waiter had just cleared their prawn and stone-crab appetizer. Lexie looked across the white-linen-covered table at Josh, his dark hair gleaming under the muted lights, his eyes resting on hers. Unable to find her voice, she jerked her head in a nod. Rising, he held out her chair, then clasped her hand in his warm palm and led her to the dance floor.

She gave herself a mental slap on the forehead. What on earth was wrong with her? She was positively tongue-tied. Here she was, dressed to the nines, at her favorite restaurant, indulging in her favorite foods, sipping delicious wine, surrounded by romantic music and atmosphere, accompanied by an incredibly attractive, attentive man who was—

Her date.

Ah. There it was. The problem in a nutshell. No matter how she might try, there was only one name for this evening, and that was *date*. And while her heart was totally in the groove and lovin' the date, her mind was screaming, *Are you crazy? What the hell are you doing dating this guy? He's another Tony—a daredevil—only instead of wearing parachutes and hiking gear, Josh wears chaps and spurs. Remember those rodeo pictures of him? Yikes! And next on his agenda is sailing the freakin' Mediterranean! And actually he's worse than Tony because in addition to being a daredevil, this guy lives a few thousand miles away. And he's going back there in a couple of weeks. Do you want him to take your stupid heart with him when he leaves?*

No, she did not. No way.

They joined a half dozen other couples on the parquet dance floor. The quartet of musicians played something romantic and slow, and Josh pulled her into his arms. While one of her hands encircled his neck, he captured the other and pressed their entwined fingers against his chest. He settled his other hand low on her bare back.

Warmth kindled at the contact, flaring into sizzling heat when his fingers slowly feathered up and down her spine. Between his caressing hand, the brush of his hard body against hers as they swayed to the music, and his clean-shaven cheek resting against her hair, she was in danger of melting into a quivering blob right on the Blue Flamingo's elegant wood floor.

"You're very quiet," he said, the soft words warm against her ear. "You okay?"

She debated lying, but couldn't bring herself to utter the falsehood. But how much of her inner turmoil and confusing feelings did she really want to admit? Raising her head from its very cozy nest on his shoulder, she looked at him and said, "To tell you the truth, I'm sort of nervous."

He instantly pulled her closer to him. "That better?"

"Actually, it's worse."

Unmistakable desire flared in his dark eyes. "I know exactly what you mean, sweetheart. You, in that dress..." He took a deep breath. "Have mercy. My willpower has never been so sorely tested. 'Cause as much as I love that dress *on* you, I can't wait to get it *off* you."

"That's funny, I was just thinking the same thing about you and that suit."

"You know what they say about great minds." He studied her for several seconds. "But I get the feelin' something else is bothering you."

"What makes you think that?"

"You've got this little pucker between your eyebrows. And your lips are pursed just a tiny bit."

Damn! She instantly relaxed her facial muscles and he smiled.

"Too late, I already saw it."

"You don't know me well enough to be able to read my expressions." *So accurately.*

"I'm pretty good at reading people. And I've spent a lot of time the past few days looking at you." He raised his brows. "Am I wrong?"

"No," she admitted in a disgruntled tone. "Sheesh. You can ride horses, cook, clean up and now decipher my expressions. Is there anything you can't do?"

"Yeah. Read your mind." He pressed his hand to the small of her back, bringing her closer against him. A sheet of paper couldn't have squeezed between them. "Tell me what's wrong."

"All right. The problem is that this is a...*date*," she whispered in an accusatory hiss.

He blinked. "And that's a problem because...?"

"We already agreed that we're not *dating*."

Understanding, along with something else she couldn't define, dawned in his eyes. "I see. We're having a *fling*."

"That's right."

"And people having a *fling* aren't allowed to eat?"

"Well, yes, they can eat—"

"Are they allowed to dance?"

"I suppose, but—"

"Touch each other?" He ran his hand up and down the length of her bare back.

She shot him an exasperated look. "You sound more like a lawyer than a cowboy."

"Took a couple of business law classes on my way to being an engineer. But I admit defeat here. Maybe you should explain to me the difference between a fling and dating, 'cause I don't get it."

"You *date* someone to get to know them. To see if you're compatible. If you inspire *emotions* in each other. To see if you want to form some sort of *relationship*. A fling is no-strings sex. Strictly physical, no messy emotions, no thoughts of the future. Just three rules: fun, wild and temporary." She nodded, relieved she'd gotten that out in the open. "Understand?"

"Yup. Now I've got it."

"Good."

"We're dating," he said at the exact instant she said, "We're having a fling."

She stared at him, speechless. He wasn't supposed to say that. While she searched for her voice, he gently squeezed her hand resting on his chest.

"Lexie. I want to get to know you. To see if we're compatible. Explore these *emotions* you inspire. See if we want to form some sort of *relationship*."

She swallowed to moisten her dry throat. "But what about no-strings sex?"

"The sex with us is great. Better than great." He hesitated, then added, "But I'm not sure that the 'no strings' part applies."

She stared at his lips, certain those words couldn't have come out his mouth. But they must have, because they echoed through her mind as if he'd whispered them directly into her brain.

He stared at her through very serious eyes. "There's something between us. Some sort of magic. More than just sex."

"How do you know?"

"Because I've had just sex. I've had flings. And believe me, this is more. And I've felt it from the first moment I saw you. I guess the question is, do you feel it, too?"

What she felt was a strong need to sit down. Darn it, this conversation was not going at all the way it was supposed to! She'd thought for sure he'd jump all over her "strictly physical, no messy emotions, no thoughts of the future" fling definition, and thereby squash this seed that had foolishly, impossibly, planted itself in her heart.

God help her, she did feel it, too. But she didn't want to.

"Josh...nothing can happen between us."

"Lexie...something already has."

Panic fluttered in her stomach. "I'm only looking for a fling—something I would think I'd have in common with a guy who's only planning to be here for a few weeks."

He studied her for several seconds then said, "Flings aren't your usual style."

"What makes you say that?"

His dimple flashed at her suspicious tone. "I meant it as a compliment. And I can tell. The fact that you were engaged. That you hadn't had sex in a year. Your house is a *home*. It's cozy and warm. Like you." His serious gaze rested on her. "Am I wrong?" When she didn't answer, he asked, "How many flings have you had?"

"Including us?"

"Yes."

"One."

Tenderness filled his eyes. "Well, I hate to tell you this, sweetheart, but you're down to zero, because this is *not* a fling."

"But it can't be anything else. No matter how attracted I might be to you, there are things about you that just make you all wrong for me to...date."

"Such as?"

"How about the fact that you live thousands of miles away from here? What about your ranch?"

"Last I heard the airlines were still operating."

"Is that what you want? A long-distance relationship?"

"No, but—"

"Well, neither do I. And that's all we could have because I'm not moving. Never again." She rushed on before he could speak. "And what about your desire to see the world and travel? My wanderlust chromosome is dead, with a capital *D*. And then there's your occupation."

"You have something against cowboys?"

"I meant the rodeo."

A frown pulled down his brows. "That's my *former* occupation. I retired, remember?"

"Yes. But you can't retire the part of your being which craved that danger, that adrenaline rush. That made you climb on the back of a two-thousand-pound, pissed-off bull that wanted to toss you into next week— after it stomped on your head. It's the same part of you that is determined to sail around the Mediterranean. Sailing is dangerous, even for experienced sailors, which you are not. And the Mediterranean is not exactly a bathtub."

He stopped dancing. "I take safety very seriously."

"I'm sure you do. But you can't control the actions of a Brahman bull and you can't control the sea."

He held her by her upper arms, his eyes steady on hers. "I'll admit I'm not the sort of man to sit around on my hands, but is that the sort of man you want?"

"The point is, I've already had the sort of man who didn't know fear. I can't go through that again."

"I know fear. At the risk of sounding arrogant, it's what made me so good at what I did. It kept me sharp and focused. I just never allowed it to overwhelm me or stop me." He cupped her face between his palms. "And if you think I don't feel fear right now, telling you I want to explore these feelings we have, you're dead wrong. I'll come right out and admit it. I'm afraid of the way you make me feel. Afraid that you won't feel the same way about me. And scared spitless that you'll let your fear overwhelm and stop you—stop us—from finding out where this could lead." His dark eyes searched her face. "Are you going to do that, Lexie? Or are you going to look that fear in the eye and kick its ass? Do you really want to ask yourself down the road what might have been?" Leaning down, he gently kissed her. "I know I don't," he whispered against her lips.

Good Lord, he could probably sell matches to Lucifer himself. She should run, not walk, away from him. From his persuasive words and compelling eyes and coaxing kisses. But she couldn't move.

Resuming their gentle swaying to the seductive music, he said, "C'mon, Miss Lexie. Let's date and see what happens." A smile curved his lips. "Sure, we like each other now, but who knows—maybe after a few dates we'll realize we really don't care for each other at all."

Fat chance. Maybe *he'd* decide that, but she had a sinking feeling that *she'd* most likely end up with her heart battered and bruised. Still, his question echoed through her mind. *Do you really want to ask yourself down the road what might have been?* No, she didn't. But fear of what could lie down the road settled like a brick in her stomach. And fear won. Darn it, she hated when that happened.

Still, did it really matter if they hung the title "fling" or "dating" on themselves? No. He'd suggested "a few dates." That sounded temporary. Temporary fling, temporary dating—as long as she remembered that the operative word was "temporary" there shouldn't be a problem. Probably.

Clearing her throat she said, "Well, since you put it that way...I'm going to kick fear in its ass. Wanna date me, cowboy?"

"Like you wouldn't believe."

9

"DATING HIM is the smartest thing you've done in years," Darla proclaimed at lunch the following afternoon after Lexie had brought her up to speed on the Josh situation.

Lexie could only stare. A good ten seconds went by before she located her voice. "What? What are you saying? You're supposed to be the voice of reason. The anchor keeping me from floating out to sea. What happened to 'repeat after me, this is only a fling'? Where's all those 'fun, wild and temporary' rules?"

Darla popped a crispy French fry into her mouth and shrugged. "I was wrong." Before Lexie could recover, Darla leaned forward and looked her directly in the eye. Or at least Lexie assumed it was directly in the eye—it was hard to tell since they both wore sunglasses.

"Look, Lexie. From everything you've told me, Josh is great—and I don't just mean in the sack, although even with your stingy lack of juicy details, I gather he is." She raised her brows for confirmation, and after Lexie nodded, Darla continued. "So you'd be crazy *not* to date him. How many handsome, thoughtful, kind, generous, polite, talented, smart, sexy guys—who are single *and* straight—and just happen to be world-class rodeo stars cross your path? Good God, woman, you've discovered a diamond in the tar pits. Thank your lucky stars and enjoy it."

"But what about the fact that he's leaving here in a few weeks?"

"Maybe if the dating goes well enough, he won't leave."

A tiny spark of hope flared in Lexie's heart, but she ruthlessly extinguished it. "Of course he'll leave. He owns a ranch in Montana. He can't just not go back. He has responsibilities."

"Just more to like about him," Darla said. "He's responsible. *And* owns his own company."

"Yeah. Several thousand miles away." Leaning back, Lexie dragged her hands through her hair. "And yes, he's great, but he's also a daredevil. Look at this crazy idea to sail the Mediterranean—"

"Lexie." Reaching across the frosted-glass table, Darla squeezed Lexie's hand. "It's really not all that crazy. In fact, based on what you told me about him and his dad, it's actually very sweet and sentimental."

"I know, but—"

"And he is taking every precaution, learning to swim and sail first. It's not as if he just jumped into a boat without any preparation."

"I know, but there's also the matter of his success. Don't get me wrong, I think it's wonderful, but you didn't see how all those people flocked around him that night we went out. Tony never even came close to that level of celebrity and look how it changed him."

Darla pursed her lips, clearly considering her words, then said, "I see your point, but just because Tony did something doesn't mean Josh will."

"I realize that. But can you blame me for being cautious? Concerned? Hell, for being scared to death?"

"No. In fact, if it were me, I'd be terrified. But the bottom line is, you're falling in love with Josh. And no one ever said love wasn't terrifying. And from everything you've told me, he's falling for you, too. You can't just throw that away without giving it a chance."

"And when my heart gets broken—what am I supposed to do then?"

"Maybe it won't get broken. Maybe you'll fall so deeply in love with each other that there won't be any obstacle you can't overcome together."

"Or maybe—and much more likely—he'll hightail it back to Manhattan and take my heart with him."

Darla nodded in commiseration. "A frightening prospect, but, Lexie, you need to look that fear in the eye and kick its ass. Josh could be *the* guy. Wouldn't it be worse to walk away now and never know? Do you really want to ask yourself down the road what might have been?"

In spite of her knotted stomach, Lexie couldn't help but laugh. "Good grief, are you sure you haven't met Josh? You sound just like him."

"No, I haven't met him. And needless to say, I'm dying to."

Lexie checked her watch. "You could get your wish. He mentioned that he might come down to the pool around lunchtime and swim some laps."

"In that case, I'm glued to my chair. Does he know you're here at the Marine Patio?"

"No. I mentioned I was meeting you for lunch, but didn't say where."

"Well, I hope he puts in an appearance soon. I can't stay much longer. I have a listing appointment at two o'clock. Which reminds me, I heard a rumor this morning that your piece of land could be coming on the market soon."

Lexie's heart stuttered. "How soon?"

"Possibly by the end of the month. I'll tell you the minute I know any..." Darla's voice trailed off, her attention captured by something behind Lexie. "Don't look now," Darla whispered, "but *the* most divine man is standing behind you, in the breezeway leading to the lobby."

"Tall, dark hair, aura of confidence, heart-stoppingly attractive but not in a pretty-boy way, body to die for?"

Darla lowered her designer shades and stared at Lexie over the tortoiseshell rims. "Oh. My. God. *That's* your cowboy?"

Lexie took a quick peek over her shoulder, noting Josh, dressed in dark blue swim trunks, beach towel casually looped over his broad, bare shoulders, making his way from the lobby toward the pool. The mere sight of him set her pulse on "flutter." "That's him."

Darla laid her hand on Lexie's forehead. "You must be running a fever. You had to even *think* about dating that man?"

Lexie lowered her own sunglasses and met Darla's incredulous eyes. "Yes. I had to think about it. Because what was supposed to be simply fun, wild and temporary has taken an unexpected and frightening turn. Because unfortunately there's more involved than just my hormones."

Darla's expression instantly changed to contrite. "Well, I can understand why." Her gaze darted back to Josh. "Good Lord, Lexie. He's—"

"Incredible. I know."

"Are you *sure* he doesn't have a brother? Jeez, I'd settle for a long-lost cousin."

"No brother, but I do seem to recall him mentioning a cousin in Texas. I'll ask him if you'd like."

"Oh, I'd like." Darla raised her iced tea in salute. "Well, here's to hoping that everything works out the way you want it to."

"Thank you. Problem is, I'm not sure I know how I want it to work out."

"Sure you do. You want that glorious man to fall madly in love with you, sweep you off your feet, and be your Prince Charming. Shouldn't be too difficult—he's already got his own horse." Her attention riveted once again over Lexie's shoulder. "What's he doing?"

Lexie turned and smiled at the trio of young boys surrounding Josh. One of them handed him a length of rope. "Looks like he's showing some young fans a few rope tricks."

They watched Josh make a lasso. He expertly twirled the rope around himself, then the children, who laughed and applauded. Josh then hunkered down on his haunches, and showed the boys how to fashion the knot.

"Seems as if he likes kids," Darla remarked with an unmistakably envious sigh in her voice.

"He does."

"Well, if your Josh is a sample of what the men are like in Montana, I know where I'm heading on my next vacation."

Lexie eyed Darla's costly off-white ensemble. "I don't think they wear Calvin Klein on the ranch," she teased.

"Maybe not suits. But Calvin makes some bitchin' jeans." Darla suddenly straightened in her seat and jerked her head to the right. "Looks as if kids aren't the only ones who want to see what your cowboy can do with a rope."

Lexie turned where Darla had indicated. A buxom blonde wearing a sarong-wrap beach skirt and a bikini top that resembled two poker chips held together by dental floss was sashaying toward Josh with an unmistakable predatory gleam in her eye. She held a piece of paper and a pen in one hand and a long-necked bottle of beer in the other. Male heads snapped in her direction as she made her way around the perimeter of the pool.

"She's looking for an autograph," Lexie murmured.

"She's looking for a lot more than that," Darla corrected. "It'll be interesting to see what she gets."

The blonde stopped in front of Josh and offered him a come-get-me smile that tightened Lexie's stomach. An image of Tony flashed through her mind, followed immediately by one of Josh with that walking sex ad wrapped around him, and she gritted her teeth. Josh straightened and nodded, giving the woman a smile. Lexie noted that his smile appeared no more than simply friendly and that his eyes didn't wander south of her chin. He signed the piece of paper she handed him, then nodded and returned his attention to the trio of small boys. The blonde said something else to him, and Lexie cursed her inability to read lips. But whatever she said, Josh shook his head in reply. With a flip of her long hair, the woman strode away.

"Looks like Blondie was shut down," Darla said in an unmistakably satisfied undertone. "Talk about not being like Tony. There's only one kind of man who says no to a woman who has 'I'm ready and willing to have wild, sweaty sex with you' tattooed across her 38-D implants."

"Yeah. A gay, dead guy."

"And your cowboy is neither of those." Darla looked her straight in the eye. "The only kind of man who can resist that sort of invite is one who is head over heels in love. Now the question is, what are you going to do about it?"

Lexie looked across the length of the pool at Josh, laughing and smiling with the boys, and her heart melted like a marshmallow over a campfire. But how could she ignore their differences? And her deep-seated fears of making the same mistake again? "I don't know, Darla. I just don't know."

"Well, if you need to talk, call me," Darla said, squeezing her hand in commiseration. "I have to go. But I want an intro to dream man first."

Lexie led Darla around the pool. As they approached Josh and his charges, he looked up. His eyes met Lexie's and a slow smile, filled with unmistakable pleased surprise and undeniable heat, lifted his lips. From behind her Darla whispered, "Good Lord. The way he's looking at you is making *me* sweat. How can you stand it?"

"Believe me, it's almost more than I can take," Lexie whispered back.

Josh rose to his feet and, after handing the rope back to the boys and ruffling their hair, he walked toward her. "This is a nice surprise," he said. Leaning down, he brushed a quick kiss across her lips, stopping her breath.

She performed a quick introduction. "Darla and I just finished lunch."

"Pleased to meet you, Darla," he said, shaking her hand and giving her a friendly smile.

"Same here," Darla said. She indicated the trio of boys with a nod. "Pretty fancy rope work there."

"Kids always get a big kick out of it. Of course, it looks a little more authentic when I'm wearin' my cowboy gear." He looked down at himself and laughed. "Whoever heard of a cowboy in a bathin' suit?"

"Not clothes you'd normally associate with a rodeo champ," Darla agreed with a grin. "But we *are* in Florida, you know." She glanced at her watch. "Much as I'd love to stay and pick up some lassoing techniques, I need to get back to work. Nice meeting you, Josh. And Lexie, don't forget to ask him about the cousin." With a queenlike wave, she departed toward the lobby, weaving her way among the lounge chairs.

Josh tickled his fingers down Lexie's arm, then held her hand. "Cousin?"

"When I told her you didn't have a brother, she wondered if you might have any unattached male cousins."

"As a matter of fact I do."

Lexie slapped her hand to her chest. "Be still, my heart. You mean there's more at home like you?"

A teasing grin lit his face. "Nah, I'm one of a kind." His gaze skimmed down her shorts and T-shirt. "Are you headin' back to work?"

"Yes. I have a scuba excursion leaving the dock at two." She wriggled her back and winced at the ache in her muscles. "Note to self—horseback riding, sailing and engaging in unrestrained sex all in the same day is not a good idea."

He lifted her hand and pressed a warm kiss against her fingers. "Oh, I don't know. Sounds like a great day to me. Still, if I had to choose only one of those activities, it would have to be—"

"Horseback riding."

He made a sound like a game show buzzer. "Wrong answer," he said in a soft voice that sent a pleasurable tingle down her spine. "And sailing is the wrong answer, too."

"Oh yeah? What kind of cowboy are you?"

"Invite me over tonight and I'll show you." He leaned down and flicked his tongue over her earlobe. "I'll even bring dinner and cook for you."

Bring dinner? A feat that would require a trip to the supermarket? *And* cook? *And* sex? Yikes. If she didn't get away from him right now, she'd never make her scuba lesson.

Stepping away from him and the potent spell he seemed to cast upon her whenever he was within a ten-foot radius, she forced a deep breath and a smile.

"All right, cowboy, you've got yourself an invite. How does seven o'clock sound?"

"Like a long time from now."

Damn it, it sure did.

AT EXACTLY SEVEN o'clock—which had indeed seemed like a long time—Josh deposited a half dozen white plastic grocery bags on Lexie's kitchen counter. Raising his chin, he sniffed the air.

"What's that odor?" he asked. "It smells like something burned."

Color rushed into her cheeks, making his fingers itch to touch her skin. "Nothing. I, um, set the oven on self-clean. It makes a funny smell."

She turned from him and tried to look in the bags, but he grabbed her around the waist, pulling her close.

"No peeking," he said.

She made a pouty face, and he laughed. "You remind me of a kid on Christmas morning."

"And you're being a Grinch. Can't I have just one tiny peek?"

He pretended to ponder her question as he backed her up until her backside bumped against the counter. "Maybe one tiny peek—but it's going to cost you."

"Name your price."

He rubbed himself slowly against her.

A wicked gleam flared in her eyes. "You drive a hard bargain, cowboy."

"That I do, ma'am. Wanna see how hard?"

"Like you wouldn't believe."

With a groan, he gave her the kiss he'd been thinking about all afternoon. She parted her lips in welcome, and he deepened the kiss, his tongue claiming the minty heat of her mouth. His hands slipped under her bright pink tank top, skimming up her smooth back. A groan rumbled in his throat. She wasn't wearing a bra.

Breaking away from her lips, he kissed his way across her jaw and down her neck while his hands came forward to cup her breasts. Her nipples tightened, pressing into his palms, and a long, low sigh of pleasure escaped her.

Every thought fled from his head. Damn, it was as if a fog of hot need swallowed him every time he touched her. Hell, every time he got near her. Aching, his erection straining against his jeans, he grasped her hips and lifted her onto the counter. Her eyes flared with arousal, and with her lips wet from their kiss, erect nipples pressing against her shirt, she leaned back on her hands and spread her legs.

He pulled down her tank top, exposing her breasts and trapping her arms against her sides. Leaning down, he took her taut nipple into his mouth, while he ran his hand up her leg and under her short, full skirt. Her panties were already damp, inciting him further as the musky scent of her feminine arousal assailed him.

Pushing aside the wisp of material, he slipped two fingers into her wet heat. A cry of pleasure ripped from her throat and she opened her legs wider, moving sinuously against his hand. She came almost instantly, and he raised his head to watch her orgasm consume her as she pulsed around his fingers.

The instant he felt her relax, however, she blew away any thought he might have entertained about her going limp in his arms. Instead she sat up and reached for the button on his jeans. "More," she demanded in a rough, smoky voice, her eyes hot. "Now. *Now.*"

He'd learned his lesson well, and pulled a condom out of his back pocket. Seconds later he thrust into her, hard and fast, wild and hungry, as if they were starved for each other. Gripping her hips, he stroked her deeply, watching himself thrust into her, then withdraw, thrust, then withdraw.

"Josh," she moaned, her body tightening around him. The feel of her, the sound and sight of her, pushed him over the edge, and his release rushed through him.

"Lexie." Her name whispered past his lips like a prayer, and he clasped her tightly against him. When he could breathe again, he leaned back and brushed a damp curl from her forehead.

"If that was the appetizer," she said in a still slightly breathless voice, "then I can't wait to see what you're cooking up for the main course."

"I don't know. At this rate, we may not eat until midnight. You're a big distraction to the chef."

She didn't look the least bit contrite. Moving against him she asked, "You complaining, cowboy?"

"Hell, no."

"Well, that's good. 'Cause I'm not finished with

you." She looped her arms around his neck and planted a noisy kiss on his cheek.

"Oh, yeah? What did you have in mind?"

"A little game."

"Well, if it's anything like the last game, you can definitely count me in. What's this game called?"

She grinned. "Doctor."

He smiled back. "I already know how to play that one."

"Excellent. Then you know the drill. Take off your clothes."

"Stick out your tongue."

She pursed her lips. "Hey! That's my line."

Lifting her off the counter, he headed down the hall toward the bedroom. "How about if we both take off our clothes, and both stick out our tongues, and see what happens?" he suggested.

Holding on tight, she nibbled on his earlobe. "I think we both know what will happen. Since I never got my peek, is there anything in those grocery bags that needs to go in the fridge?"

"Nope. I bought a bag of ice that's in with the perishables. And that should prove just what sort of cowboy I am."

"The smart kind?"

"That, and the Boy Scout kind. Always prepared." Walking into the bedroom, he deposited her on the bed, then set about removing his clothes. "You'll note I had a condom in my pocket."

"That was a very smart—and much appreciated— move."

"Yeah? Well, Miss Lexie, then hang on, because my clothes are off and I think you're going to appreciate my next move even more."

WEARING NOTHING except Josh's denim shirt, Lexie patted her mouth with her napkin.

"That steak was delicious. The potato, green beans, and salad, too. You're a great cook."

"Glad you liked it. Wait till you see what I have planned for dessert."

Lexie groaned. "I couldn't eat another thing."

"Don't worry. It's not that kind of dessert."

"Oh." Their eyes met across the width of her kitchen table and she couldn't help but smile at him. Garbed in only his boxer briefs, he was a very distracting dinner companion. Distracting and entertaining. Watching him prepare dinner, she'd learned that there isn't much that is sexier than a nearly naked man slaving over a hot stove.

"Why don't you go relax in the hot tub while I clean up?" she suggested. "I'll meet you out there."

"Why don't I help you clean up, then we can go relax in the hot tub together."

"But you cooked. You shouldn't have to clean up, too."

"I'd rather be in the kitchen with you than out in the hot tub alone."

Good Lord, this man was going to kill her. Reaching out, she captured his hand. Bringing it to her mouth, she gently nibbled on his index finger, then sucked it into her mouth. His eyes seemed to glaze over and he shifted in his chair.

"You keep doin' that, darlin', and these dishes will stay right here."

"Hmm," she hummed against his fingers. "And that would be really bad, right?"

He chuckled. "I think I sense a bit of the procrastinator in you."

"Only when it comes to housework," she stressed, peppering his fingers with kisses and flicks of her tongue. "Especially laundry. I do it, but I hate it." She eyed him with speculation. "I don't suppose you like to do laundry?" Nah. He couldn't be *that* perfect.

"Can't say that I like it, but it's one of those things that's got to get done—so you just do it."

"Ah, but I have this very interesting theory about laundry," she said. "Would you like to hear it?"

"Love to—but I'd love it more if you'd sit on my lap while you told me."

Releasing his hand, she rose, then resettled herself by straddling his lap, facing him. "You see," she explained, slowly trailing her fingers down his bare chest, "if everyone would just get naked, there'd be no need for clothes, and thus, no need for anyone to do laundry ever again. Think of the ramifications. Think of all the time we'd save never having to shop for clothes. All the money we'd save not having to buy clothes. All the money we'd save on food. With everyone running around naked, you'd want to be in the best shape possible, so everyone would eat less, thereby saving on groceries." She tickled her fingers over his ridged abdomen and he sucked in a breath. "Of course, the whole idea would only work if *everyone* did it."

"You sold me. Let's test it out right now."

She raised her gaze from the fascinating ribbon of hair bisecting the skin below his equally fascinating navel. "Huh?"

"Let's get naked." He unsnapped her shirt with one firm tug, then immediately leaned forward to take her nipple into his warm mouth.

Heat shot through Lexie and she arched her back. "I thought you wanted to clean up."

"Later. Right now I want you." He cupped his hands on her buttocks, pulling her tighter against his erection. "Any complaints?"

"Absolutely not."

"Unfortunately the condoms are in the bedroom."

"Except for this one." Smiling, she pulled a plastic package from the pocket of his denim shirt, then dangled it between her fingers. "Slipped it in there before dinner. Boy Scouts aren't the only ones who know how to be prepared."

His clever fingers stroked between her splayed thighs and her eyes slid closed. "Let me light the fire," he whispered against her ear.

"I...mmm...don't have a fireplace."

"Darlin', it's not that kind of fire."

BY THE TIME they got around to the dishes, the remains of dinner had hardened on the plates. Lexie cleared the table, while Josh loaded the dishwasher.

"What's this?" he asked, pulling an aluminum foil-wrapped plate out from behind the coffeemaker.

"Nothing!" Lexie made a grab for the foil, but he was too quick. Before she could stop him, he'd unwrapped the plate and was staring at the contents.

Embarrassment scorched her cheeks. He said nothing for several interminable seconds, then he finally raised his gaze to hers and regarded her with an impossible-to-read expression.

"You made these?" he asked. "For me?"

"Well, I *tried* to. You'd mentioned that chocolate-chip cookies were your favorite. I gave it my best shot, but clearly I should have just stopped at the bakery." She shook her head. "I told you I was a lousy cook."

"So *that's* what I smelled earlier."

"I'm afraid so. I was going to trash them, but you arrived, and then I forgot."

His brows shot upward. "Throw them away? Why?"

"In case you haven't noticed, I burned them." Her gaze wandered to the flat, charred disks on the plate and she winced. "Incinerated is actually closer to the truth."

He picked up one of the scorched cookies, brought it to his lips, then took a big bite. He chewed slowly, his gaze never leaving hers.

Her stomach tightened in sympathy and she prayed his act of chivalry wouldn't cause him any gastrointestinal distress.

He swallowed, God bless him, but then to her amazement, he took another bite. Clearly the first bite had killed off all the poor man's tastebuds.

She reached for the plate, but he held it protectively against his chest. "Josh, please, you don't have to eat them. They're awful."

"No, they're not."

"They're not?"

"Nope." His lips curved into a smile so filled with warmth and delight, her breath caught. "They're just like Mom used to make."

THE NEXT MORNING, after their early morning sailing lesson, followed by a swimming lesson during which Lexie merely swam laps alongside him, Josh let himself into his hotel room.

Dropping his key onto the still perfectly made bed, he walked into the bathroom and turned on the shower. After washing off the chlorine, he closed his eyes, braced his hands against the tiles, and let the warm water rush over him as images of Lexie danced behind his eyelids.

Lexie smiling at him over a glass of wine. Her pleasure over the dinner he'd made her. Laughing as he'd fashioned a mini lasso from a piece of yarn and played with Scout. Sighing with pleasure as he'd massaged away her lingering aches from their horseback riding lesson. Crying out his name in release. Her soft skin under his hands as she fell asleep in his arms.

Two more weeks. He was scheduled to leave here in two more weeks. The mere thought of it cinched his stomach into knots. How the hell could he? He couldn't. Yet neither could he stay. He had responsibilities back home. A ranch to run. People who depended on him. And he had a quest to finish. Damn it, he was going to sail a boat in the Mediterranean. He had to. If he didn't, it would eat at him till his dying day.

She was the thing that was messing up all his nice, neat plans. Falling in love with her was wreaking havoc with his life, blowing him to bits in the emotional minefield he'd laid himself.

Every minute he spent with her, every time he touched her, spoke to her, shared a memory with her, made love to her, another bomb detonated. And to top it all off, she'd baked—okay, burned—him chocolate-chip cookies. Because he'd mentioned they were his favorite. That sweet, simple gesture had cut him off at the knees. Indeed all her actions and gestures showed that she cared about him, and she'd agreed that they were "dating," but she hadn't given him any other verbal indication that he meant anything more to her than a fling. And he was running out of time. And patience.

He knew what he wanted. He wanted Lexie. He wanted her to fall in love with him. He wanted them to figure out a compromise to remain together after his time at the Whispering Palms ended.

He just wasn't sure about the best way to go about getting those things to happen.

Shutting off the water, he grabbed a towel. Wrapping the white terry cloth around his waist, he wiped off a section of the steamy mirror with his hand then stared at his reflection. "Why the hell couldn't you have fallen in love at some other, more convenient time? And maybe with a gal who lived a little closer to home? One who wanted to travel? And one who didn't look spooked every time you mentioned the word 'rodeo'?"

When his reflection remained silent, he left the bathroom. The phone rang and he snatched up the receiver.

"Hey, Josh. It's Bob," came his business manager's voice. "How's the vacation? You all rested up?"

"Vacation's going great," he said, not adding that sleep was playing a minimal role.

"And how about those sailing lessons?"

"Just fine."

"Glad to hear it. Listen, I'm calling 'cause I just got the heads up on something I think you'll find very interesting."

Josh tilted his head back and looked at the ceiling. He had a strong sense he knew what was coming next. And he didn't want to hear it. "Bob, I'm retired."

"I know it." A lengthy pause filled the air. "But Wes Handly isn't."

The mention of his rival's name piqued Josh's curiosity, as he knew Bob had hoped. "I'm listening."

"Handly's just signed on for an international charity event in Europe scheduled for next month. Right now he's the biggest name on marquee. But I know another name that could knock him off the top spot." Before

Josh could reply, Bob rushed on, "The corporate sponsors are going nuts with this, Josh. They're promising the moon if you'll step out of retirement. Not only would it make you rich—"

"I'm already rich."

"You can never be too rich. Besides, this event will not only raise a load of money for charity, it would give you a chance to compete against Handly again. To hand him the loss he should have had last time. To let you go out on top, where you belong."

Damn, as much as he hated to admit it, Josh couldn't deny that the thought of going head-to-head against Handly one more time, to have another chance to beat him, made his blood hum with anticipation. He should have won that last competition. Coming in second still rankled.

"When do you need to know?"

"Sponsors want to set up a meeting as soon as possible, in Miami. Josh, listen, this is a once in a lifetime opportunity. Don't pass it up. Handly's talking about retiring himself next year, so this would be your only chance. Grab it with both hands. And, just as a bit of added incentive, I thought I'd point out something you may not have considered—this event takes place in Monaco."

"So?"

"Monaco is on the Mediterranean."

Josh mulled that over for about ten seconds, then mused out loud, "So I could tie up two bulls with one rope."

"Practically with one hand tied behind your back," Bob agreed. "And collect a big fat paycheck to do it."

And then he'd be free, his quest over. Free to concentrate his time and energy on his future. And Lexie.

"Bob?"

"Yes, Josh?"

"Sign me up."

There was no missing Bob's sigh of relief. "Atta, boy. I'll tell the sponsors right away, and call you back with the details. This is going to be great, Josh. You made the right decision."

Josh ended the call several minutes later then stared at the phone. He didn't doubt he'd made the right decision—he'd wanted another crack at Handly since the day he'd hung up his spurs. And with this event taking place in Monaco, with the Mediterrean spread at his feet, well, surely that was some sort of sign.

Yet he couldn't banish the niggling doubt at the back of his mind. In spite of knowing he'd done the right thing for himself, he strongly suspected that Lexie would take a dim view of him coming out of retirement. Her opinion of daredevils was crystal-clear: she wanted no part of another one. She already thought his sailing quest was dangerous, so him taking part in this rodeo would definitely convince her that he was indeed a daredevil. The same sort of man she'd already broken off an engagement to. Would she banish him from her life in a similar way?

No! No, he wouldn't—couldn't—let that happen. He'd find a way to make her understand. But, just to be on the safe side, best not to mention it until Bob had all the arrangements in place, the contracts signed, and all systems were go. No point telling her about it now in case the plans somehow fell through. Better to wait, until everything was set in stone. Then he'd tell her.

Hell, he'd even invite her to come along! He could see them now, strolling the streets of Monaco, sailing together, her sitting in the arena, watching him trounce Handly.

Yes, indeed, that was a very good plan.

She won't understand, his inner voice interjected, souring his rosy fantasy. *You're going to end up like the fiancé—dumped on your ass as if a bronc bucked you.*

Raking his hands through his still damp hair, he ruthlessly squashed the voice. She *would* understand.

Somewhere in the back of his mind, he heard, *Ha!*

He managed, with a great deal of effort, to ignore it.

_____ **10** _____

WITH THE MIDMORNING SUN warming her back and the calm, clear turquoise water glistening with bright shafts of sunlight, Lexie stood on the resort dock, waiting for her next group of snorkelers to arrive. After double-checking that the gear was all ready, she sucked in a deep breath, then exhaled in what could only be described as a contented sigh.

The three days since she'd burned Josh his chocolate-chip cookies had whizzed by in a blur of happiness. Thanks to the exceptional weather, she and Josh continued their lessons by sailing the resort's sixteen-foot sailboat each morning for an hour before her shift began. He was learning fast, which didn't surprise her one bit. She could easily see him excelling at anything he set his mind to.

During the day, while she worked, Josh spent his time swimming and driving around to look at sailboats and sailing schools. She occasionally saw him in the afternoons, at the pool or on the beach, sometimes alone, sometimes chatting with other guests or entertaining a child. Several times she noted him challenging other pool swimmers to a race. He might not ride in the rodeo any longer, but his competitive spirit was clearly still alive and kicking. When he saw her he'd wave and wink, or blow her a kiss as she led a group snorkeling or to the dock for a scuba excursion. She'd wave back, knowing that in a matter of only a few hours, she'd be with him again.

They'd spent each evening together, once going out for dinner, twice cooking at her house. He taught her the finer points of "cowboy cuisine," such as to how to grill a steak and ribs, and she taught him how to burn toast and scorch pizza. He taught her how to make s'mores on the grill, and she taught him some really interesting uses for melted chocolate.

Josh bought her a beautiful cowboy hat, which she felt sort of odd wearing until she realized how much it turned him on—especially when she wore it and nothing else. Last night, after dinner, he'd taken her to the movies, but when he'd offered to see a chick flick no less, her eyes had narrowed with suspicion.

"Okay, what's wrong with you?" she'd asked.

"Nothing," he'd said, his face a mask of innocence.

She'd remained unconvinced—he couldn't be that perfect—and was soon proved right when she realized that it wouldn't have mattered *what* movie he'd taken her to since they sat in the last row and Josh wouldn't keep his hands or his lips to himself. She missed most of the show—not that she was complaining...

And the nights...magical, passionate nights spent in Josh's arms. Endless hours indulging in sensual exploration, learning, touching, talking, laughing.

A long sigh escaped her. She'd never, not even with Tony, felt like this. Had never imagined she *could* feel like this. She loved being with Josh. Loved seeing him smile and hearing him laugh. Loved watching his eyes twinkle with mischief, then darken with arousal. Loved seeing him interact with the fans—especially the children—who invariably found him at either the resort or the several restaurants they'd ventured out to. In fact, she loved everything about him.

She loved him.

The realization slammed into her like diving into the water and landing with a belly flop. This wasn't just physical attraction or infatuation. She was *in love* with Josh.

She stood on the dock, staring at the water, and rubbed her hand over the spot where her heart beat hard and fast.

Surely the realization should panic her. At the very least, distress and worry her, but instead only exhilaration rushed though her.

She shook her head. She must be losing her mind. She should *not* be happy about this. She was *not* supposed to fall in love with a fling, with her transition man. All the reasons they were wrong for each other flashed in her mind. He was temporary. A daredevil. Lived thousands of miles away.

But her heart bulldozed the reasons aside, visualizing the house she wanted to build on the peaceful cove she coveted—and right smack in the middle of her house stood Josh, smiling, arms open, waiting for her. She wanted him there, in her house, with her, sharing her life.

Closing her eyes, the words *I love Josh* washed over her like a warm rain. She loved him. Completely.

But what do to about it? They hadn't discussed the future, or the fact that he was scheduled to leave the resort in less than two weeks. It seemed that by some unspoken mutual agreement, they'd avoided the subject, but his rapidly approaching departure sat between them like a scowling Victorian chaperone.

Their time together was slipping away, yet how

could she allow their relationship to simply end in a matter of days? She couldn't. But it wasn't just a matter of what *she* wanted. What did Josh want? Did he care for her as she cared for him? There was no doubt he enjoyed her physically—did his feelings run deeper than that? That night at the Blue Flamingo he'd hinted as much, but he hadn't broached the subject again.

Well, there was only one way to find out. Ask him. Ask how he felt. Ask if he wanted to try to figure out a way to make this work. Because the thought of him just leaving, of this being over, simply did not compute.

Perhaps this very subject was what he wanted to discuss with her? He'd left the resort at 10:00 a.m. to drive to Miami to meet with his business manager and several corporate sponsors. She'd walked him to his car and before driving off, he'd said, "Let's have dinner at your place tonight so we can talk."

Well, she was ready to talk. Ready to lay her cards on the table and tell him how she felt. Ready to hear him say he felt the same way. Ready to figure out a way for them to be together. Ready to work out a compromise so that could happen.

She could only pray he was ready to do the same.

JOSH STOOD on Lexie's porch and took a deep, calming breath. Damn, he felt as nervous as a mouse wearing catnip perfume. *Settle down. Everything's going to be fine.*

But his mental pep talk did nothing to soothe his jangled nerves. Everything he wanted was inside this cozy house. And he was determined to have it. He just hoped the lady would agree.

If he'd been capable of laughter, he would have chuckled at himself. Even when facing the most ornery of bulls, he'd never felt this unsure or frightened. Well, he'd faced those bulls down. How much trouble could one small woman be?

Setting his jaw, he knocked. Seconds later Lexie opened the door, wearing a sultry smile.

And nothing else.

He actually felt his eyes bug out of his head. Good damn thing his jaw was attached to his head or else it would have hit the ground.

Reaching out, she grabbed his hand and pulled him inside, closing the door behind him. Leaning back against the oak panel, she waggled her brows at him.

"Hiya, handsome."

He cleared his throat to locate his missing voice. "You're naked."

"Now that's what I like about you. Your superior powers of observation. Must come with the chemical engineer territory. But in this case you're wrong. I'm wearing cologne."

He shifted to relieve the strangulation occurring in the front of his jeans. "What if I'd been the mailman?"

"I knew it was you. I saw your car in the driveway." She erased the several feet between them with a sinful sway of her hips. When she stood directly in front of him, she walked her fingers up the front of his shirt, then pressed herself against him.

"Anytime you'd like to set down those grocery bags and give me a proper hello would be fine with me," she whispered against his neck.

The bags hit the tile. With a groan, he crushed her against him, fusing his lips to hers in a hot kiss that left them both breathless.

"I missed you all day," she whispered against his mouth while her fingers yanked open his shirt snaps. "Wanna know how much?"

"Yeah." The single word came out as a groan when she rubbed her breasts against his bared chest.

She turned them in a circle, until his back pressed against the door. His heart pounding, ragged breaths burning his lungs, he watched her sink to her knees. Slipping the button free on his jeans, she carefully eased down his zipper. He sucked in a breath of relief at the removal of the tight denim constricting him—a breath that was sharply cut off when she freed his erection and took him slowly into her mouth.

A long groan vibrated in his throat. Tunneling his fingers through her soft hair, he watched her pleasure him, absorbing the erotic sight of her lips gliding over him, the incredible feel of her tongue circling him.

His head dropped back, bumping against the door. It was too much, yet not enough. He couldn't take any more, yet his body craved, demanded more. More of her. Wrapped around him. Skin to skin. With a growl, he pulled her up, then turned her so she stood with her back braced against the door.

Quickly rolling on the condom from his back pocket, he cupped her buttocks in his palms and lifted her. She clasped her legs tightly around his hips and he slid into her wet heat. Sweat broke out on his brow and he gritted his teeth against the pleasure, wanting to sustain it, knowing he was helpless to do so.

"Do you suppose," she panted, her face flushed, eyes dark with need, "that someday you'll come over and we'll actually make it to the bedroom?"

"Not much chance of it if you open the door naked, sweetheart." He slid nearly all the way out, then glided deep, eliciting a purr of pleasure from her.

His orgasm was fast approaching, cutting off his ability to speak. He increased his tempo, reading her body with a knowledge born of many hours spent in sensual exploration. Seconds later she tightened around him and he let himself go, his release shuddering through him with a ferocity that left him barely able to remain standing.

A good minute passed before any sound save their choppy breathing filled the air. Finally he lifted his head from her fragrant neck and looked at her.

Her hair lay in frantic disarray, looking as if she'd been struck by lightning. Her skin glowed from the exertions of their lovemaking and her full lips were moist and slightly parted. Her eyes slid open and he found himself looking into slumberous hazel depths that sent a jolt straight to his heart.

A grin lifted one corner of her mouth. "I definitely think I should put a sofa in this foyer."

"Might be a good idea. Probably should think about one in the kitchen, too." He glanced down at the bags on the floor. "I think the eggs broke."

"What did you need them for?"

"I was hoping for an invite for breakfast."

"You're invited. And don't worry about the eggs." She shot him an exaggerated leer. "I'll have 'Josh over easy' for breakfast."

"Honey, you've already got 'Josh scrambled.' Seeing you open the door like this—" his hands gently squeezed her bare butt "—I don't know if I'm comin' or goin'."

"Hmm. Well, tell you what. You feed us, then we'll 'go' to bed and I'll show you all about 'coming.'"

"Sounds like a plan. And I can vouch that you give good lessons, Miss Lexie."

She ran her finger over his bottom lip and adopted a prim, schoolmarmish expression that would have proved more convincing had she not been naked and still wrapped around his hips. "Of course I give good lessons. I *am* a teacher."

"That's perfect. 'Cause I'm more than willing to learn."

LEXIE WATCHED Josh all through dinner, and as the meal progressed, it became increasingly obvious that something was troubling him. He picked at his food and was uncharacteristically quiet. He caught the conversational ball when she tossed it, but he wasn't throwing out any first pitches. She knew he planned to talk to her about something—and she'd hoped that that something was good news. Good news about their future. Good news about a way they could work things out and be together. But his silence and the way he avoided her eyes made those hopes die a slow, withering death. A knot formed in her stomach, growing until she couldn't force down another bite. Finally she set down her fork.

"Josh, what's wrong?"

He looked up and met her gaze with a troubled expression, a fact that edged further unease down her spine.

"Nothing's wrong," he said. Setting aside his napkin, he added, "But we definitely need to talk."

Her stomach executed a maneuver that would have impressed even the most finicky of Olympic judges. Not just *we need to talk* but *we DEFINITELY need to talk.* The addition of that adverb did not bode well at all.

Forcing a lightness into her voice she was far from feeling, she said, "I'm listening."

"We've sort of avoided the subject, but we both

know I'm scheduled to leave here soon. And...I've got to go."

Another stomach triple somersault. "Back to Manhattan."

He hesitated. "Not exactly. Although I will have to go there." Reaching across the table, he clasped her hands. She forced herself not to avert her gaze from the bad news she clearly read in his expression. Whatever he was about to say, she wasn't going to like it. Knew it wasn't *we're going to be together*.

"I've accepted an invitation to take part in a rodeo next month."

Nope. That definitely wasn't *We're going to be together*. Damn it, she hated it when she was right. His statement reverberated through her mind, the ramifications striking her like openhanded slaps. She swallowed to wet her throat and dislodge the lump that had settled there.

"You're coming out of retirement." Was that flat, lifeless voice hers? Yup, sure was. And here she sat, with the Michael Jordan of rodeo. Numbness crept into her limbs. How many times had Mike unretired himself now? Two? Three?

"Yes, I'm coming out of retirement." And then, for a man who had remained mostly silent since she'd greeted him at the door wearing nothing other than cologne, Josh turned into a regular chatterbox, talking in excited tones about an international rodeo event in Monaco, and how this was his big chance to best the man to whom he'd come in second place during his final competition.

Lexie listened with half an ear, absorbing enough of the details to know what was going on, but not really interested in much past the fact that he was going back to the rodeo. To the danger. To a lifestyle where he was a celebrity—and all the trappings that came with that. But mostly to the danger. And by God, he looked so happy about it! His eyes practically glowed when he spoke about having another shot at beating this Wes Handly.

"And what makes this even better news," Josh said, squeezing her hands, "is that Monaco is on the Mediterranean. While I'm there, I can take my sail."

She could only stare. "*Better* news?" she echoed once she located her voice. "How is that better? So maybe you'll drown instead of getting stomped to death by a bull?" Stark fear, mixed with a dose of anger, seeped into her veins, taking the place of the numbness that had invaded her. "Josh, you are nowhere near ready to sail the Mediterranean."

"You're right." Before relief could set in that he at least realized that, he added, "So come with me. Help me sail. Enjoy the rodeo. Think what a great time we'd have together. It would be like a vacation."

Her entire body went cold. For a few seconds she couldn't even take air into her lungs. It was as if all the oxygen had left the room. But then a sense of frigid calm settled over her. She eased her hands from his and looked him straight in the eye.

"Vacation? Great time? Exactly what part of it would be great? Traveling? As you well know, I have no desire to travel. Watching you risk your life riding in the rodeo? The mere thought of it scares me to death and makes me feel ill. Risking my life as well as yours sailing the Mediterranean? I know how to sail, but I'm not expert enough to consider such an undertaking, especially with an inexperienced crewmate."

"Lexie, I—"

"I knew it," she said, shaking her head. "I must have

been out of my mind to get involved with you. How stupid could I have been to believe for even a millisecond that you'd stay retired? Wouldn't constantly crave danger and thrills? Once an adrenaline junkie, always an adrenaline junkie." She narrowed her eyes at him. "When exactly did you make this idiotic decision?"

Annoyance flared in his eyes. "It isn't idiotic—"

"We're going to have to agree to disagree on that one. *When?*"

A muscle in his jaw jumped. "Three days ago."

Three days ago. She didn't know whether to laugh or to cry. Or to scream. "And you're just getting around to mentioning it now." A humorless laugh escaped her. "Why did you bother to tell me at all? Oh, let me guess! You knew how I'd react, and you didn't want to do anything that would upset the sexual applecart before it was absolutely necessary. Makes me wonder why you didn't just wait a few more days—toss out the info on your way to the airport."

He jumped to his feet. Slapping his palms on the table, he leaned over her, his eyes flashing with a combination of anger and frustration. "Damn it, Lexie, that's not fair. I didn't tell you until now because the plans weren't firmly set until today's meeting. There was no point in worrying you about it until I'd signed the contracts and it was a done deal."

She looked up at him. Was it possible to actually feel your heart breaking? "You're absolutely right. There was no reason for you to discuss any of your future plans with me."

"There's every reason. I just didn't want something that might not have even happened to come between us—"

"Before it was absolutely necessary," she finished for him.

He straightened, then raked his hands through his hair. "Yes. But when you say it like that it makes it sound dishonest, and I wasn't being dishonest."

"Of course not. You were simply withholding the truth to protect me. To spare my feelings and to keep me from worrying."

His expression turned wary. "Somehow this is starting to sound like one of those 'does this dress make my ass look fat' girl-trap things."

She waved her hand in a dismissive gesture. "Not at all. You were being honorable."

"I was trying to be, yes."

"And of course, you didn't want our fling to end any sooner than it had to."

Grasping her upper arms, he pulled her to her feet. "This is *not* a fling," he said through clenched teeth.

"Not anymore," she agreed. "This fling is officially flung." She pulled in a deep breath, not sure how much longer she was going to be able to hang on to her anger and not crumple like a house of cards in a windstorm. "Look, Josh, we had some good times, but we both knew this was temporary, that anything long-term was impossible."

"It is *not* impossible. We can—"

"No. We can't. Nothing has changed. We live thousands of miles apart. You have responsibilities in Montana, and my life is here. And even if, by some miracle, we could solve the geographic problems, I can*not* live with this decision you've made. There will always be another rodeo, another reason to come out of retirement and risk your life. Or if it's not a bucking bull, then some other dangerous enterprise like sailing the seas will tempt you."

His serious dark eyes still simmered with annoyance. "I can't deny that the rodeo is dangerous, but your job isn't exactly danger-free, either."

An incredulous sound gurgled in her throat. Before she could utter a word, he plunged on, "Don't you think there are dangers associated with what you do? People are injured water-skiing and on those Jet-Ski things all the time. And parasailing? You don't think there's an element of danger in that? And even experienced swimmers can drown in rough water or get caught in an undertow. How about scuba diving? You could run out of air, or get attacked by all those dangerous things in the ocean—like sharks."

She resisted the urge to look heavenward. "This is *Florida.* There are 'things' in the ocean, including sharks."

"Exactly. And like Brahman bulls, sharks are dangerous. Can't be controlled. Can't anticipate them. Maybe they don't seem so bad to you because you're used to them. But for a cowboy from Montana, sharks are damn dangerous. Sure, a bull might break your leg, but he won't *bite it off.*"

She shook her head. "It's not the same."

"It *is* the same." He gently squeezed her shoulders. "Every time I see you going off in that boat for a scuba excursion, my gut gets tight. But I wouldn't ask you not to do it."

"And I haven't asked you not to enter this rodeo or forgo your sail. You made the decision you needed to make. I understand that. You've asked me to go with you and be a part of that decision. I can't."

"You're afraid." The gentle understanding in his voice nearly undid her.

"Josh. You could so easily be hurt. Maimed. Killed. And for what? All I know is that the last man I loved couldn't stop seeking higher thrills, and his success changed him. I lost the sweet guy I fell for to a lifestyle filled with travel, danger, hangers-on and groupies. You ask me if I'm afraid? No. I'm terrified. Of what coming out of retirement could do to you. And of what going through that again would do to me."

All vestiges of annoyance drained from his eyes. "Lexie. I'm not some green kid goin' on the circuit for the first time. I'm beyond all that. I've already sowed my oats. My head's not about to be turned by some groupie. And I swear to you, on my honor, that this is the last time I'll come out of retirement. I won't—"

She pressed her fingers to his lips, cutting off his words. "Please don't make promises you might regret later. I'm not asking for them. I don't want them. But I've already been through this with Tony. I cannot, *will not*, go through it again."

"I'm not Tony."

"Different man, same placing-myself-in-danger situation. I refuse to again put myself through the horrors of waiting for the call from the hospital that you're hurt. Or worse."

"That's not going to happen."

"You don't know that. And it's not a chance I'm willing to take."

He dragged his hands down his face. "Lexie, I could get hurt walking across the street."

"True. But you cannot deny that the odds of injury increase substantially when bucking bulls are tossed into the mix."

"You're asking me to choose."

"No, I'm not. I'm bowing out."

He studied her through troubled eyes. "Lexie, this rodeo and sailing are things that I *have* to do. To have peace with myself. They'll be finished in a few weeks. You and I will have all the time in the world after that."

"No, we won't. We're out of time." She moved around to put the kitchen table between them, then glanced down at the cold remains of her half-eaten dinner. A shudder ran through her. Was it less than an hour ago that they'd sat down to this meal? Just over an hour ago that they'd made love in the foyer?

"I understand your concern," he said in a quiet voice, "but why can't you trust me? I'm doing the right thing."

She forced herself to meet his gaze. "Yes, you are. For you. And that's fine. I just don't want to be involved with it in any way. You have every right to do what you think is best. And I have every right to be afraid and unwilling to risk myself again."

"We can work this out, Lexie. More than anything, I want to be with you." He reached her in two quick strides, then clasped her shoulders and gently shook her.

She stared at him and pretended her heart was still beating. He wanted to be with her—but not more than he wanted to ride in the rodeo. Shaking her head, she blinked back the hot tears welling in her eyes. "Don't say that."

"Why not? It's true." His eyes searched hers. "The question is, do *you* want to be with *me?*"

Looking into his eyes, she swore she heard her heart splatter onto the floor. "It doesn't matter. There's no future for us."

"There could be if—"

"If I was able to accept your decision regarding this dangerous rodeo and taking your sail before you're prepared, which I'm *not*. If I was capable of setting aside my fears, which I clearly am not. If I was willing to risk my heart and happiness and future on another man who could very well destroy all three—and I'm *not*."

"You're scared. I understand, but—"

"I'm more than scared. More than terrified. I'm adamant. I can not, will not, do this again. *Never* again."

His face paled. He slowly released her shoulders, a muscle jerking in his jaw, his eyes clouding over with anguish. Before he could say anything else, something that might threaten her resolve, she wiped her face clean of expression and raised her chin. "I want you to leave."

The most deafening silence she'd ever heard filled the room. His eyes seemed to burn into hers and she spent those silent seconds memorizing his face feature by feature, yet knowing he was already permanently emblazoned in her memory. She wanted, needed, him to go. Now. Before the pain bubbling inside her exploded.

After what seemed like an eternity but was probably no more than a minute, she repeated, "I want you to leave, Josh. *Now*. Do you understand?"

His lips flattened into a hard line. "You've left precious little room for misinterpretation." He dragged his hands down his face, then shook his head. "I don't know how to say goodbye to you."

"Then don't say it. Just go. Please." Her voice broke on the last word, and she fisted her hands in an effort to keep herself together.

He stared at her for another few seconds, his throat

working. Then he walked swiftly from the room, the sounds of his boot heels hitting the ceramic tile echoing through the house. She listened to the front door close with a quiet click. Seconds later she heard his car backing out of the driveway. And then silence.

He was gone. Completely. Irrevocably. Forever.

Her knees went limp and she sank into her chair. Nothing. She felt nothing. The place where her heart used to beat in her chest felt anesthetized. Indeed, her entire body felt as if it had taken a direct hit of Novocain.

Something wet landed on her arm, and as if in a trance, she looked down. A drop of water. As she stared at the spot, another drop fell. Then another. Tears.

A sob rose in her throat, accompanied by a blinding rush of heartache that bordered on physical pain, and she wished for the oblivion of her previous numbness. Because he was gone. And nothing had ever hurt this much.

11

"YOU HAVE *GOT TO GET* yourself out of this funk," Darla said two weeks later, striding into Lexie's kitchen, her arms laden with the fixings for margaritas and nachos.

"I'm not in a funk," Lexie lied, listlessly following Darla's energetic form.

Darla plunked her supplies on the counter and immediately made herself at home, dragging the blender out of a lower cabinet. "Well, if you're not in a funk, then you're doing a hell of an imitation of it. And since you wouldn't come out and party with me, I brought the party to you. Tonight it's just the three of us—you, me and—" she patted the bottle of tequila "—José Cuervo."

"I would have gone out, but I've been busy."

"Busy moping. The same as you've been for the past two weeks." Reaching out, Darla gave Lexie's hand a sympathetic squeeze. "I know you're hurting, Lex, and that's why I'm here. I'm the Official Un-Funker, De-Moper. After a few margaritas, fattening snacks and girl talk, you'll feel better. And look at this." She handed Lexie a folded section of newspaper. "There's a huge beach gear show at the convention center next week, guaranteed to draw lots of eligible men. We're going. The best cure for a broken heart is a new man. And you're not going to find one hiding out at home."

"I'm not interested in finding a new man, Darla. In

fact, if I never see another man again, it will be too soon."

"Oh, boy, that statement proves you're still in Phase One of a breakup," Darla said, her eyes filled with concern. "I *know* we shouldn't have waited this long to have a heart-to-heart. I should have yanked you out by your hair the minute Josh left town. And I would have if you'd answered your phone."

Proud that she didn't even wince when Darla mentioned his name, Lexie said, "I got your messages. I called you back."

"Yeah, and left messages on my machine saying you were fine. Which you are not. Two weeks after the guy is gone, you should have moved on to Phase Two. Maybe even Phase Three."

Lexie didn't ask what Phases Two and Three entailed—it didn't matter, she didn't care, and she wasn't up to doing them, whatever they were. Unless they were crawling into bed with the remote and a drowning-the-sorrows pint of double-chocolate-fudge ice cream. If so, she was in.

"I really am okay, Darla. Just busy. I've been putting in a lot of extra hours before and after work, giving private swimming and scuba lessons."

"I'm glad. But one look at you and it's clear to me—who knows you very well—that you're operating on autopilot. And it's high time you reengaged your gears. And to help you do that, I have some good news for you. But I'm not going to tell you until the nachos and 'ritas are ready. So go turn on the TV, or read a book or something while I get busy."

"I could help," Lexie offered, dubiously eyeballing the packages of meat and seasonings.

"Lex, the last time you helped, you burned the nachos." She made shooing motions with her hands. "Go."

Heaving a resigned sigh, Lexie walked into the living area, plopped down on the sofa, then flicked on the tube. She mindlessly channel surfed, trying unsuccessfully to push from her head the one thing that occupied every corner of her mind.

Josh.

Damn it, how long before she stopped hurting? Before this crushing ache lessened so it didn't feel as if an elephant sat on her chest? Before she stopped thinking about him several hundred times a day, in turns recalling their time together, then wondering what he was doing—and the even more agonizing, Who was he doing it with?

The high-pitched whirl of the blender sounded from the kitchen, and she grimaced. Yup, that's just what she felt like—as if she'd jumped heart-first into an ice-cube filled blender then pushed Frappé.

The aroma of spicy meat filled the room, but did little to interest her. She stared blindly at the images blinking past on the screen as she clicked the remote without enthusiasm.

Well, this pain had to lessen soon. It *had* to. All she had to do was to stop thinking about him. Stop recalling his smile. His laugh. Stop calling to mind the feel of his hands on her body, the texture of his skin against hers.

Stop seeing him on TV.

Her fingers froze on the remote and she stared at the image of Josh. Her gaze flicked to the bottom corner of the screen, noting by the logo that this was one of those nonstop sports channels. Heart pounding, she upped the volume.

"In other sports news," came the commentator's voice, "Josh Maynard won the International Charity Rodeo held earlier today in Monaco. Maynard, winner of the most All-Around Cowboy titles in history, came out of retirement for the event. He bested rival Wes Handly, who came in second."

As the commentator spoke, footage showing Josh atop a bucking bull flashed. Lexie's breath stalled as she watched what the sportscaster called a "brilliant" ride. Then the picture changed to a grinning Josh, holding a huge gold belt buckle above his head, circling slowly around the center of the arena, waving to a wildly cheering crowd.

"Here's your drink," said Darla, setting a colorful plastic glass on the glass-top coffee table. She plopped next to Lexie on the sofa, then pointed toward the TV. "Hey! Isn't that Josh?"

Unable to speak around the lump in her throat, Lexie nodded. He looked wonderful. And happy. And uninjured—thank goodness. Aching loss raced through her. If only things had been different—

But they weren't. It was over between them.

The program switched to baseball and Lexie turned off the television.

After several seconds of silence Darla asked, "You okay?"

Lexie took a shaky breath. "To tell you the truth, I've been better."

"The fact that he won the competition...maybe that means he'll come back and—"

"No," Lexie interjected more sharply than she intended. "It only means that he fulfilled one of his goals. I'm happy for him and wish him all the best. I'm even glad I saw his moment of glory on the TV. But his goals and mine are light-years apart. It's over."

"But—"

Lexie's vehement head shaking halted Darla's words. "No buts. Now, what's this good news of yours?"

It was obvious from Darla's expression that she didn't want to change the subject, but, after heaving a dramatic sigh, she said, "I had lunch today with a Realtor friend whose broker has been contacted by the owner of the property you're interested in. If all goes well, the land will be on the market very soon. Maybe within the next few days."

For the first time in two weeks, a spark of interest stirred in Lexie. "How much?"

Darla named the asking price and the spark of interest flared into real hope.

"Believe it or not, I can actually swing that!" Lexie said.

"You'll need to move fast," Darla warned. "I understand from my friend that other buyers have shown an interest. We'll make a written offer and, hopefully, the owner will accept it right away. If so, you'll have your half acre of heaven." She handed Lexie her margarita. "And something to keep your mind occupied."

"Something to keep my mind occupied would really be welcome," Lexie admitted before she could stop herself.

Darla jumped on the opening like a flea onto a hound. "I'm so sorry things didn't work out for you and Josh. I feel sort of responsible. After all, I'm the one who urged you to go for it."

Knowing she couldn't forever avoid having the "Josh conversation" with Darla, Lexie decided to bite the bullet and just get the ordeal over with. "You didn't urge me to do anything I didn't want to. And it's certainly not your fault that he's gone."

An image of Josh, staring at her just before he left her house, flashed through her mind. It was the last time she'd seen him. When she'd arrived at work the next morning, she learned that he'd checked out of the resort late the previous night.

She should have been relieved, glad his early departure had erased any chance of running into him again, forcing an awkward confrontation or conversation. Instead it had felt as if she'd been sucker punched in the heart.

"Still, I feel like I talked you into dating him," Darla said, her eyes troubled.

Lexie gave Darla what she hoped passed for a reassuring smile. "Look, I'm twenty-eight years old. A big girl. I have no one to blame but myself for the heart bruise. I knew going in he wasn't right for me, but I stupidly followed my heart instead of my head."

She sucked down several long mouthfuls of margarita. "Well, never again. I've made the same mistake *twice*. Now it's time to make a different mistake. I'm not sure what that mistake will be, but one thing's for damn sure—it will *not* involve another adrenaline junkie. If the guy so much as rides a bicycle without a helmet, he's history."

"That's the spirit," Darla said approvingly. "The fact that you're talking about another guy means you're inching toward Phase Two. Now all we need to do is find you some sexy guy to have a fling with and you'll be all set."

The word "fling" hit her like a cold, wet washcloth. The mere thought of another man touching her made her feel queasy—or maybe that was just from her free-dom with the margarita on an empty stomach. Still, it seemed as if every pore ached with missing Josh.

She mentally thunked her forehead. Josh. Josh. Josh. How to erase him from her mind? Her heart? Being at home was torture—memories of him filled every room of her house, yet, except for work, she could barely stand the thought of going out. And work offered little refuge since every time she looked at the pool or the beach—on average a few hundred times a day—she visualized Josh swimming or walking along the shore.

Damn it, it was time to crawl out of this self-imposed exile. She'd mourned long enough. She hadn't heard a word from Josh—not that she'd expected to. But lying awake in her empty bed during the long nights, she hadn't been able to extinguish the foolish hope flickering in the deep recesses of her heart that he might call or write.

Well, clearly he'd moved on with his life, and based on his obvious happiness on the TV, he was thriving. Now she needed to do the same. Surely this breath-stealing ache would diminish with time.

And as for a man? Phooey! She didn't want or need a man cluttering up her life. And that was fine—she didn't have to have one. But it was time to pull herself up, dust herself off, and start living for herself again.

"I'm not ready for a fling, but I'm ready for *me*," she said out loud, her head swimming a bit from the potent drink. "Who needs Josh anyway? With him gone, it's one less bell to answer, one less egg to fry."

"No offense, Lexie, but you don't know how to fry an egg."

"Well, I'm going to learn. And I'm going to buy my

piece of land and build a house on it. And stay right here in Florida. And be happy, damn it. *Happy.*"

Okay, her head—marinated though it was in margarita—was convinced. Now she just had to work on her heart. And she'd do that. As soon as she found all the pieces.

JOSH STOOD in the center of the arena, listening to the thunderous applause. Accepting the gold buckle, he held the trophy above his head and circled slowly. Wes Handly, who'd come in second, tipped his hat, and Josh returned the gesture of mutual respect. He circled again, absorbing the moment, recording it in his memory, storing it alongside all his other great rodeo memories. And that's exactly what they were—memories. Now officially part of his past.

"Stick a barbecue fork in me, I'm done," he murmured to himself. He'd beaten Wes, and he could leave the arena for the last time with no regrets. It was time to start making some new memories. And he knew exactly where and with whom. He just needed to tie up a few loose ends, and then the rest of his life could begin.

With a final wave he exited the arena, pausing to shake Wes's hand.

"That was a great run, Josh," Wes said. "You gonna give me another shot at you?"

"No way. You're on your own. I'm restin' on my laurels."

"And your bruised ass," Wes said with a laugh.

Josh grinned. "It ain't as bruised as yours."

"True." Wes settled his Stetson back on his head. "A bunch of the boys are headed out to one of them fancy casinos. Wanna join us?"

"No, thanks. I've got other plans."

"Oh, yeah? Blonde, brunette or redhead?" Wes asked with a knowing smile.

"Bright red. And she's real sleek and trim and fast. Just the way I like 'em."

"What's her name?"

"*The Quest.*"

Wes grimaced. "That's a heck of a name for a woman."

Josh slapped Wes on the back and grinned. "I reckon it would be. But it's a real nice name for a sailboat."

LEXIE SAT in her kitchen, listlessly dunking her tea bag up and down in her favorite yellow ceramic mug. A shaft of sunlight fell across the kitchen table, and a sigh escaped her. Here it was, a beautiful morning, blue skies, warm sunshine and her day off—and she was utterly miserable.

She looked down at the burned fried eggs on her plate. What sort of culinary curse afflicted her that she couldn't cook an egg without it coming out of the pan looking like a hockey puck? She'd offered the blackened mess to Scout who had reacted with a feline hiss of outrage and a baleful glare at Lexie.

Her glance wandered toward the calendar hanging on the cream-colored wall next to the refrigerator and another sigh eased past her lips. He'd left exactly one month ago today.

An entire month. Damn it, why did she still hurt so bad?

Because you love him, you jerk, her pesky inner voice chimed in.

Damn, she hated that inner voice. It never shut up. And it was always right. How annoying was *that*?

All right, she loved him. But surely the feeling would

go away soon. Wouldn't it? *Nope*, said her inner voice with brutal honesty.

Great. Her love for Josh was going to stick around like a bad rash. What she needed was an antidote for love. Like serum for a poisonous snakebite.

How was it that her breakup with Tony—a man she'd loved and had planned to marry—hadn't come close to hurting like this.

Because you didn't love Tony the way you love Josh. Because with Tony you knew you'd done the right thing and this time you're not so sure.

Okay, the damn voice had to go. In an effort to shut it up, she pulled the newspaper toward her and flipped through the pages. A small item on page ten caught her attention: Swimmer Suffers Shark Bite. She scanned the words. A fifteen-year-old boy required seventy-two stitches to close a wound to his calf when a shark attacked him the day before in the shallows off a beach about ten miles from the Whispering Palms.

Josh's words came back to her in rush. *Sharks are dangerous...a bull might break your leg, but he won't bite it off...every time I see you going off in that boat for a scuba excursion, my gut gets tight. But I wouldn't ask you not to do it.*

A frown pulled down her brows. Maybe he'd had a point. Maybe her job did involve some danger. But surely nothing like climbing onto the back of a pissed-off, two-ton bull. Every time her mind replayed the TV footage of him riding that beast, the butterflies in her stomach grew queasy.

The phone rang and, relieved to have her thoughts interrupted, she reached over to snag the handset from the counter. "Hello?"

"Lexie, it's Darla."

Her heart fluttered at Darla's voice. Could this be the call she'd been hoping for? She'd made her offer on the piece of land yesterday, but she hadn't expected to hear back so soon. "Do you have news?"

"I do."

Even though Darla only spoke those two words, something in her tone skittered dread down Lexie's spine. "Please don't keep me in suspense."

"I'm afraid that the owner accepted another offer, Lexie. I'm so sorry."

"Another offer?" she echoed in confusion. "But I offered the asking price!"

"And unfortunately another buyer offered more."

"Well, I'll just make another, even higher, offer," she said, her mind frantically trying to calculate how much more she could afford to spend.

"There's nothing we can do. The owner has already accepted the other offer."

This could not be happening. Lexie pressed her palm against her forehead in a vain effort to stem the throb setting up behind her eyes. "Maybe the other deal will fall through?" she suggested in a hopeful voice.

"That is, of course, always a possibility," Darla said slowly, "and I would certainly let you know, but I don't want you to get your hopes up, Lex. The other buyer is paying cash, so the deal can close quickly. Within a few weeks."

"I see." She felt like a balloon someone had just let all the air out of. "Who's the buyer?"

"I don't know...but does it really matter?" Darla asked, her tone gentle and sympathetic.

Darla had a point. "No."

"Listen. I'm going to scour the listings and we're going to find you another piece of land. A better piece. I'll print out some possibilities today at work, then we'll go out for dinner tonight and look them over. There's a lot of land for sale in Florida, Lex."

True. But she'd only wanted one, tiny piece of it. One tiny *specific* piece. And now it was gone. "Thanks, Darla, but—"

"No buts. We're going out tonight and that's final. I'm showing up at your door at six sharp. Wear something sexy, because after dinner we're hitting a few clubs."

"But—"

"No *buts.* The only excuse I'll accept is if you already have a date with Ben Affleck. Do you?"

"No." The word came out as a snarl.

"Then chin up, and I'll see you at six."

Before Lexie could say another word, the dial tone sounded in her ear. Clicking off the phone, she closed her eyes, then dragged her hands down her face.

She wanted to cry, to scream out her frustration, maybe even get up and smash a coffee cup or two, but she remained dry-eyed, silent and seated, trying to come to grips with the numbing, knee-buckling fact that her dream of building her house on *her* cove was gone.

She wasn't certain how long she stared off into space before the insistent ringing of her doorbell roused her. She rose and made her way to the door on leaden legs. With the way her luck was running, this was probably someone coming to tell her that her car had fallen into a sinkhole.

But what the heck. Her heart was broken, her land was gone, and she forgot to apply sunscreen yesterday so her damn nose was peeling. How much worse could this day from hell get?

She pulled open the door and instantly discovered the answer.

A whole lot worse.

12

LEXIE STARED at Josh, standing on her porch. Josh with his weight propped on a pair of crutches, his right leg wrapped from the knee down in a cast, and a hell of a shiner surrounding his right eye.

What on earth had happened? When she'd seen him on TV, he'd been fine. Had he competed in another rodeo?

She ruthlessly cut off the barrage of questions and gave herself a mental slap. *Not your problem, Lex.*

Yup, what a relief this guy was no longer on her radar screen—him and his cast and crutches and bruises. 'Cause if he *were* still on her radar screen, her stomach would be clenching and her heart thumping at the sight of his injuries. And she didn't feel the least bit clenched or thumped. Nope. Not a bit. And the fact that she couldn't find her voice around the lump in her throat? Just an aberration. And that moisture pushing behind her eyes? Just the fact that she hadn't dusted lately.

Raising her gaze from his cast, their eyes met. Dozens of memories she'd thought she'd sorta, kinda, almost filed away under "the past" bounced through her mind. Damn it, why did he have to darken her doorstep and resurrect those images she'd worked so hard to bury?

A sheepish half grin pulled up one corner of his

mouth, flashing that damn sexy dimple. "Are you going to invite me in?"

She wanted to say no. Wanted to slam the door in his face, to shut him out of her life and mind. Whatever his reason was for blowing through town and stopping by and flashing his dimple, she didn't want any part of it. Because he would just leave again. How many times was she expected to bear the pain of saying goodbye to him?

Raising her brows, she lifted her chin and forced a coolness into her voice. "I suppose I'd better invite you in. If I don't you might lose your balance on those crutches and topple into the flower bed." She stepped back to give him room to enter the foyer.

"Thanks." The rubber tips of his crutches sounded a soft *splat* against the ceramic tile.

"Would you like some coffee?" she asked, closing the door, trying her darnedest to ignore her traitorous heart, which seemed to thump out in Morse code, *He's here! He's here!*

"Coffee would be great."

She followed him into the kitchen, absolutely not noticing how at-home he looked in her house, instead forcing herself to note the fact that he handled himself on those crutches like a pro. No doubt due to lots of past practice from a long line of rodeo-related injuries. Yup, good thing he was no longer her problem. She might love him, but that would fade in time.

Yeah, like in a hundred years, her inner voice snickered.

While he settled himself in the kitchen chair he'd always occupied during their *fling*, she measured out scoops of fragrant grinds into the filter. Why was he here? And why didn't he say something? She at least had a reason for her silence—the big lump blocking her throat. What was *his* excuse?

She added water, then switched the coffeemaker on. Unable to put it off any longer, she turned around and faced him. Their eyes met. Just looking at him, her heart tumbled down to her toes, taking her stomach and a few other vital organs along for the ride.

When he still remained silent, annoyance trickled through her. Whatever he wanted, it was time he spoke up. Then left her alone. And clearly she was the one who was going to have to get things moving along here.

She cleared her throat. "So you injured yourself in the rodeo. I have to admit, I'm having a very hard time not saying 'I told you so.'" Humph. Take *that* and stick it in your Stetson, hotshot.

"Didn't get hurt in the rodeo."

She pointedly eyed his cast. "Slipped on the deck while sailing the Mediterranean?"

"Nope. I fell at the airport. Here. Last night. Tripped over my damn duffel bag." He leaned forward, resting his forearms on the table. "Was all your fault, I'll have you know."

Her eyes goggled. "*My* fault? That *you* tripped?"

He nodded solemnly. "I'd set down my bag to dig out my cell phone. I was dialing your number when, through the windows, I saw this gal getting into a cab. I didn't see her face, but she had your curly brown hair. I thought it was you—"

"It wasn't."

"I realized that when she turned her head, but unfortunately I'd already started forward. I tripped on my duffel and went down like a hog-tied calf. What followed was more embarrassing than anything I've ever faced. People all gatherin' around and starin', then the ambulance arriving. Talk about feeling like the south end of a horse." He shook his head. "I spent the whole friggin' night in the emergency room getting X-rayed and outfitted in this cast. Definitely *not* the way I'd hoped to spend the evening. I would have called you, but I, uh, know how you feel about getting calls from the hospital. So I waited until I was discharged, and...here I am."

"Yes, here you are." Looking big and vital and wonderful, albeit bruised, making her heart perform acrobatic leaps. "May I ask *why* you're here?"

Without taking his gaze from her, he slowly rose, then hobbled toward her. He stopped when only a foot separated them, then leaned forward, bracing his hands on the countertop on either side of her, caging her in. She pressed her backside harder against the counter, but there was no escaping, unless she wanted to give him a shove. Given the facts that he was injured, and her traitorous body was very happy to have him standing so close, she opted against the shove. Instead she gazed into his serious eyes and prayed he couldn't hear her heart pounding.

"I'm here," he said in a low, husky voice, "because this is where *you* are. And where *you* are, is where *I* want to be."

Elation and something akin to panic collided in her. Clearly he wanted to continue their fling. And while her body and mind were all for it, her heart wanted no part of the inevitable battering it would receive when he left again. And damn it, she resented that he obviously believed he could just pop into town and drop by. As if they were still involved. As if their fling hadn't ended.

Forcing a calm detachment that surely deserved an

Academy Award, she said, "Is that so. And how long are you in town for *this* time, cowboy?"

His gaze never wavered. "That depends."

"On what?"

"You."

The intensity of his gaze burned her. Heat emanated from his body and although he hadn't touched her, she still felt scorched. His clean, masculine scent filled her head, notching up her temperature another few degrees. She had to resist the urge to fan herself.

No doubt about it, he was potent, and his nearness was nearly impossible to resist. It would be so easy to fall back into his arms, to touch him and to be with him, to resume their fling. But nothing between them had changed.

She raised her chin. "I fail to see how I would affect the length of your stay. Our relationship ended a month ago."

"No. A month ago, I had to leave. Now I don't have to. Unless..."

"Another rodeo comes along?"

"No. Unless you want me to. And even then, I gotta tell ya, you're going to have a hell of a time gettin' rid of me."

A flicker of hope sparked in her chest, but she ruthlessly extinguished the tiny flame like a blown-out candle atop a birthday cake. "Look, Josh. I'm not interested in another temporary fling."

Whatever reaction she'd expected from him, it certainly wasn't the relief-filled smile that relaxed his features. "Well, now that's exactly what I wanted to hear. 'Cause I'm not interested in another temporary fling, either. And not to put too fine a point on it, but I believe we'd agreed at some point that we were *dating*."

"And it didn't work out. And nothing about our situation has changed. I don't understand—"

"Oh, but *everything* about our situation has changed," he broke in.

"Really? How do you figure that?"

"Well, for starters, I've hung up my spurs for good." Clearly her doubt showed, for he added softly, "And I can only ask that you take my word on that, Lexie. I don't make promises I can't keep, and my rodeo days are done. Not because I have to, but because I want to. I beat Wes Handly in Monaco, and set a new record while I was at it. I'll always love the rodeo, but it's time to move on." His gaze rested on hers. "To other things I love."

Her heart and breath seemed to stall. Good thing her lungs knew how to operate on their own, because all her faculties appeared frozen.

"While I was in Monaco, I rented a sailboat," he continued. "Hired myself an experienced captain, and spent an entire day sailing around the harbor. Under his watchful eye, I operated the boat, then I let him take over while I just watched the water and thought about how much I wished my dad was with me and how he would have loved being there."

The sorrow in his eyes tugged at her and she briefly touched his upper arm. "I'm sorry he wasn't, Josh."

A sad smile lifted his lips. "Me, too. But I accomplished what I'd wanted to, and in my heart, I know my dad was with me in spirit. It's another chapter now officially closed."

Tenderness filled her. "I'm glad your sail and your rodeo victory brought you the peace you sought."

"They did. The entire trip taught me a lot. Like about the whole travel-the-world thing." A sheepish expression crossed his face. "That was really more my dad's dream than mine, and to be perfectly honest, I think I've seen enough of it for a while. I'm not a big fan of the jet lag, and going places isn't much fun when you're going by yourself."

"But you were surrounded by rodeo people!"

"Yeah, but that isn't whose company I wanted." His gaze searched hers. "I missed you, Lexie."

Splat. Great. Her heart just fell onto the floor.

Before she could fashion a reply, he reached out and gently traced the tip of his index finger across her cheek. "I missed you so much, I couldn't stand to be away from you any longer. So here I am. For as long as you want me."

She blinked twice, certain this was a dream and she would wake up and find herself alone. But he remained standing in front of her, dark eyes watching her intently. She swallowed to moisten her throat. "What about your ranch?"

"That's the reason I didn't return here sooner. I had to go back to Montana and settle my affairs there. My ranch is in very good hands, being run by men I trust. I'll need to travel back there once every few months, not only to keep an eye on things, but because it's in my blood." He cupped her face in his hands. "But you're in my blood, too. And I was hopin' you'd agree to come with me when I visit the ranch. We could split our time between here and there. I think you'd learn to love Manhattan and the ranch as much as I do."

"What exactly are you saying?" she asked, no longer able to douse the hope his words ignited.

"I'm saying that I want to be with you. That I've taken steps to solve our geographic problem. That I like it here in Florida. I like ridin' horses on the beach in the morning, swimming in the afternoon and sailing in the evening. I like sharing all those things with you." His thumbs skimmed across her cheeks. "Lexie, my mother, who was a very wise woman, told me something I've never forgotten. She said that in our lives, we have only one true love. Everyone else is either practice or a substitute."

"And which one am I—practice or substitute?"

"Neither."

That softly spoken word hung in the air between them. Lexie's heart, which had miraculously risen from the floor, beat so hard she could hear the thump in her ears.

Good Lord, she needed to sit down. She locked her knees to keep from slithering onto the tiled floor. Because unless she was losing her marbles—which was definitely a possibility—Josh had just told her he loved her.

Cautiously she asked, "You love me?"

"Like you wouldn't believe."

Holy cow. She wasn't losing her marbles! "When did you realize you loved me?"

His brow puckered. "Can't say that I can pinpoint the exact moment I knew, but it was pretty early on."

"Before you left for the rodeo?"

"Well before. In fact, I was in over my head pretty much from the get-go."

She raised her brows and tapped her foot. "You didn't tell me so."

"I wanted to, had planned to that last night we were together, but things didn't go as I'd hoped. Before I knew what had happened, I found myself standing in a deep hole. And when you find yourself in a hole, the first thing to do is stop digging."

Clearly another pearl of cowboy wisdom. "So you left."

"Yeah. Timing is everything in the rodeo, and I could see that nothing I said at that point in time would change your mind. But I knew I'd be back as soon as I'd taken care of the things I had to do—things that hopefully would change your mind. And that the timing would now be right." Easing his hands from her face, he braced his weight on one palm against the countertop, then entwined the fingers of his other hand with hers. "I've laid all my cards on the table, Lexie. What I need to know is how you're going to play your hand."

A wave of love swamped her, nearly drowning her in its wake, filling all the spaces that had remained empty since he'd left. And for the first time since he'd walked out of her house, her heart didn't feel as if it were breaking.

Taking a deep breath, she managed a shaky smile. "Nothing fancy about my hand, cowboy. You've proven yourself a man of integrity, and I'll trust your word on the rodeo issue, although I will keep an eye on you to make sure you don't take up any other activities that are too dangerous. You're living proof that success doesn't have to change a person for the worse, and that a love of competition is different from being an adrenaline junkie. And also that a person can get hurt—" her gaze bounced between his cast and his shiner "—just doing everyday things."

She raised a none-too-steady hand and rested it against his clean-shaven cheek. The feel of his warm, firm skin beneath her palm shot a tingle up her arm. "Swimming, sailing and riding horses with you, visiting Montana with you, all sounds...perfect. *With you* sounds perfect. I love you," she whispered. "So much I can hardly stand it."

With a groan he leaned forward, kissing her with a passion and longing and heated possession that stated even more clearly than his words how much he wanted her. His lips left hers, blazing a hot trail along her throat. She tipped her head back, reveling in the sensation of his lips igniting her skin.

"So I guess this means we're officially dating again, huh?" she murmured, tilting her head to give him easier access.

Josh halted his exploration of her fragrant neck as a frown yanked his brows downward. Straightening, he looked at the woman he loved. She stared at him through heavy-lidded eyes, her skin flushed, her lips moist from their kiss.

"Lexie, I don't want to date."

She blinked several times. Confusion, along with something else that could only be described as wariness, replaced the arousal in her eyes. "You...you don't?"

"Hell, no. The dating thing just didn't work for us, so I vote we skip it. Let's get married."

He may have seen a more dumbstruck expression before, but he'd be hard-pressed to name it. She looked as if he'd just suggested they ride bareback all the way to Manhattan.

"Married?"

Amused by her stunned reaction, he leaned forward and touched his lips gently to hers. "Yeah. Married. You know—you, me, a minister." He leaned back and waggled his brows at her. "A honeymoon."

She didn't smile. Instead her very serious gaze

searched his. "Are you sure you're ready for that kind of commitment?"

He rested his hand over his heart. "I am fully ready to be committed." His words brought a flash of amusement to her eyes. "And," he continued, "to show you just how serious I am, I brought you this." Reaching into his back pocket, he slipped out an envelope and handed it to her. "Open it."

She cocked a brow. "Odd shape for an engagement ring," she murmured with a mischievous grin. She pulled out the contents and scanned them, her expression turning to one of utter bemused confusion. "I don't understand," she whispered. "How...?" Her voice trailed off and she shook her head.

"That day we went horseback riding on the beach," he said hesitantly, sudden doubt assailing him. Damn, she looked pale and about ready to drop. Had he made a big mistake? "You said you wanted to live on the water. Then you pointed out a spot with some great waterfront property. Said there was a whole series of canals and hidden coves and that it was peaceful and private and perfect. I spent a good bit of time driving around, looking the area over."

He touched the signed sales contract between her fingers. "That particular lot appealed to me the most. It's real quiet, with lots of trees and situated on a deepwater cove. I spoke to a broker who told me it wasn't for sale yet, but that he expected it to come up on the market soon. When it did, the broker called me and I made an offer." She just stared at him, increasing his unease. "So, uh, I bought it. Just today. Thinkin' you might like it."

Her bottom lip trembled, and a fat tear rolled down her pale cheek. His insides froze with panic. "Whoa," he said, patting her awkwardly on the back. "Hey, don't do that. If there's one thing I can't take, it's a crying woman."

"I can't believe you did that," she said, the tears coming faster.

"Me, either." He looked frantically around for some sort of tissue, and grabbed the closest thing—the dishtowel resting on the countertop—and gently dabbed at her wet cheeks. "*Please* stop crying. I'll talk to the broker. There must be some way out of the agreement. Shouldn't be a problem, especially since there was someone else interested in the land."

She made a noise that sounded like a laugh, but surely wasn't since tears still streamed down her face. "Me," she said, thumping herself on the chest like Tarzan. "*I'm* the someone else who was interested in buying it."

He stopped mopping her face. "You're joking."

"I'm not. I've been waiting for ages for that cove plot to come on the market. And just before you arrived here, Darla had broken the news that someone—someone who I promptly wished a flea infestation upon—had outbid me." An incredulous laugh escaped her, and she flung her arms around his neck, nearly unbalancing him.

"You are the most wonderful, romantic, thoughtful man," she said, covering his face with kisses between words. She leaned back in the circle of his arms and beamed at him. "I'm overwhelmed."

"Well, that's a relief. And now, you'd better hope that your flea-infestation wish doesn't come true, 'cause I have no intention of being any farther away from you than *this*—" he pulled her closer and smiled "—for a long, long time."

She wriggled against him, inspiring a groan of want in him. "You won't hear any complaints from me," she murmured.

"Glad to hear it. But you haven't officially answered my proposal." He looked into her beautiful, love-filled eyes. "So what do you say, darlin'—wanna be my cowgirl?"

She treated him to a slow, sexy smile that nearly stopped his heart. "Like you wouldn't believe."

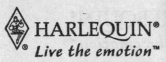

They're strong, they're sexy, they're not afraid to use the assets Mother Nature gave them....

Venus Messina is...
#916 **WICKED & WILLING**
by Leslie Kelly
February 2003

Sydney Colburn is...
#920 **BRAZEN & BURNING**
by Julie Elizabeth Leto
March 2003

Nicole Bennett is...
#924 **RED-HOT & RECKLESS**
by Tori Carrington
April 2003

The Bad Girls Club...where membership has its privileges!

Available wherever

◆ HARLEQUIN®

Temptation.

is sold....

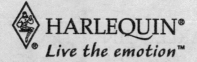

◆ HARLEQUIN®
◆® *Live the emotion*™

Visit us at www.eHarlequin.com

HTBGIRLS

We've been making you laugh for years!

 HARLEQUIN®

Duets™

**Join the fun in May 2003
and celebrate Duets #100!
This smile-inducing series,
featuring gifted writers and
stories ranging from amusing to zany,
is a hundred volumes old.**

This special anniversary volume offers two terrific
tales by a duo of Duets' acclaimed authors.
You won't want to miss...

Jennifer Drew's You'll Be Mine in 99

and

The 100-Year Itch by Holly Jacobs

With two volumes offering two special stories every
month, Duets always delivers a sharp slice of the lighter
side of life and *especially* romance. Look for us today!

Happy Birthday, Duets!

Visit us at www.eHarlequin.com

HD100TH

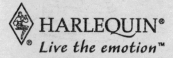